JULIE MILLER

PROTECTIVE INSTINCTS

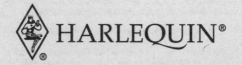

HARLEQUIN®

TORONTO • NEW YORK • LONDON
AMSTERDAM • PARIS • SYDNEY • HAMBURG
STOCKHOLM • ATHENS • TOKYO • MILAN • MADRID
PRAGUE • WARSAW • BUDAPEST • AUCKLAND

For my reading and writing students. Thanks for
keeping me on my toes and being such cool kids
to work with. Remember, each of you has a talent.
Learn something new every day—it keeps your brain
healthy and makes life more interesting. Make a
difference every day—in big ways or small, others will
appreciate it, and you'll feel good about yourself.
Keep working hard. And thanks for the chocolate!

ISBN-13: 978-0-373-88844-3
ISBN-10:   0-373-88844-9

PROTECTIVE INSTINCTS

ABOUT THE AUTHOR

Julie Miller attributes her passion for writing romance to all those fairy tales she read growing up, and shyness. Encouragement from her family to write down all those feelings she couldn't express became a love for the written word. She gets continued support from her fellow members of the Prairieland Romance Writers, where she serves as the resident "grammar goddess." This award-winning author and teacher has published several paranormal romances. Inspired by the likes of Agatha Christie and Encyclopedia Brown, Ms. Miller believes the only thing better than a good mystery is a good romance.

Born and raised in Missouri, she now lives in Nebraska with her husband, son and smiling guard dog, Maxie. Write to Julie at P.O. Box 5162, Grand Island, NE 68802-5162.

Books by Julie Miller

CAST OF CHARACTERS

Sawyer Kincaid—This gentle giant discovers a darker side to his personality when his father is murdered. When the woman who once rejected his love is targeted by a killer, will it bring out this Kansas City cop's protective instincts, or send him over the edge?

Melissa Teague—As a young woman, she married a man who turned out to be her worst nightmare. When her ex escapes from prison, she learns that putting her faith in another man may be the only way to survive.

Richard "Ace" Longbow—Melissa's abusive ex. He's escaped from prison to save his own neck from an inside hit, but what's his plan for life on the outside?

Benjamin Teague—A bright, happy four-year-old who knows nothing about the father who never claimed him. Melissa wants to keep it that way.

Fritzi Teague—Melissa's mother.

Hank Brennerman—Ace's cellmate. He likes to talk.

Tyrell Mayweather—An enemy of Ace's from inside the pen. But escaping from prison makes strange allies.

Riley Holt—The FBI agent in charge of recapturing the fugitives.

William Caldwell—Longtime family friends of the Kincaids.

John Kincaid—Deputy commissioner of the K.C.P.D. Sawyer's father. Unforgivably, unmistakably dead. But why, and who's responsible?

Prologue

John Kincaid touched his tongue to the coppery tang of his swollen split lip. His words were slurred, his confusion evident. "Who are you? What do you want from me?"

"You're a cop. Does it make any difference?" Dark eyes reflected delight in their power over him.

"Shut up! We're not supposed to talk." The one with the colorless eyes shoved the taller man.

"Back off!"

Not good. His enemies were fighting between themselves now. With his wrists handcuffed behind the rusting steel office chair, John sat helplessly in their path, waiting to bear the brunt of their discord.

"Quit playin' us! You think we're stupid, old man?"

Three of the fingers on his right hand were

already broken when the kick came and crushed another joint. John gritted his teeth, his agonizing scream growling inside his throat.

He'd been tortured like this before, having the crap repeatedly beat out of him, as though pulverizing the muscles and bones would loosen the tongue. But he'd been a young man then. Age and too many years on a desk job had weakened his body if not his will. It was harder to stay awake this time, harder to detach his brain from the violence so that he wouldn't reveal something he shouldn't.

Only, that's what made no sense. These two bastards—the hotheaded one with the prison tattoos and the older, more calculating one with the meaty fists—hadn't asked him one sensible question beyond verifying his name and position as deputy commissioner of KCPD.

Nothing about an open case.

Nothing about revenge for someone he'd killed or put away over the span of his thirty-year career as a cop.

Nothing about using him as a get-out-of-jail-free card, exchanging one of their buddies for his release.

Nothing but pain and punishment.

John hadn't recognized either man when

they'd abducted him from his Sunday-morning run through the park earlier in the day and brought him to this run-down brick-and-steel warehouse. He didn't recognize the place, either, though it was near the Missouri River—judging by the wash of water outside the walls, which his ringing ears had detected when he'd first regained consciousness in the bare-bulbed circle of light just outside the warehouse's office.

He still couldn't put a name to a face or case beyond Jaw-Smasher, as he'd silently dubbed the big black man, and Bone-Crusher, as he'd nicknamed the wiry smart-ass with the white, nearly shaved, hair.

Senseless violence was not a foreign concept to a man who'd been a cop for thirty years, and who'd served in military intelligence before that. But his kidnapping hadn't been random. These two knew his running schedule, knew the park, knew at just what stretch of road he'd be alone and out of sight from any other joggers. And they'd come prepared—with some kind of knockout drug that had taken him down before he could put up much of a fight, and a van that John had spotted and dismissed earlier on his run. Real plates. Real business logo. Woman driver.

John's awareness sharpened a notch and he slyly tilted his chin to peer through his one good eye into the broken shadows and empty spaces of the warehouse around him. Where was the woman now? Was she part of this? A girlfriend? Running the show? Another flunky? Or had she already become a victim?

John risked another question. "Where's your driver? Is she okay?"

The punch that hit his temple knocked over his chair and John turned his swirling brain and battered cheek into the cool concrete floor, letting the oblivion swallow him up.

When John awoke, he was alone. The lightbulb had either burned out or been turned off, and he was sitting upright again. Only the moonlight creeping through the broken panes of glass on the windows high above him offered any reprieve from the darkness.

Crap. Susan would be freaking out by now. Not only had he missed their Sunday date night, but he hadn't called her—hadn't been able to. During his ride in the van, his phone had been taken, along with his gun and badge. Throughout the thirty-seven years of their marriage, Susan had always insisted that he call if he wasn't going to show up when and where he was supposed to. It was the least he could do for a woman who'd been married to a cop for as long as she had. A woman who loved him, a woman who'd done the lion's share of raising four sons he couldn't be prouder of.

She'd have called those four sons by now. Three of them, at any rate. One of them might not be answering his phone this week. Not if he was on another bender. Maybe the other boys would be too busy to answer. Maybe Su was alone and frightened and he couldn't do a damn thing about it.

Outside the brick walls, a dog whined from some alley in the distance. The howl was mournful and weak, as though the animal was on its last legs, as though it was all alone and had given up hope. John turned his ear toward the sound. "I hear ya, pal," he slurred. "I hear ya."

Damn. Deputy Commissioner John Kincaid cursed the downward spiral of his thoughts and shifted, trying to ease his busted ribs and aching conscience into a more bearable position. *Concentrate.* He wasn't ready to leave his family. He wasn't ready to quit being a husband or father.

Did his wife know how much he loved her?

Would his sons remember the lessons he'd taught them?

His boys were all cops—just like him. All of them as protective of their mother as they were the people of Kansas City.

Despite their overachieving schedules, despite their own problems, they'd take care of her. Even if he never got out of this senseless hell, John knew she'd be taken care of. Believing in that one thing was the only comfort he could find.

But somebody ought to help that dog.

And a drink of water would be nice.

Some aspirin would be helpful.

Freedom would be even better.

The silence of the place hurt his ears. His battered fingers and numb arms made a token effort to escape the cuffs, but there was little his weakened body could do.

He was bleeding inside already. He knew the signs.

Unless a miracle stepped out of the shadows and freed him, he was going to die. He only wished he knew why.

And then an outside door opened. John's pulse quickened as he heard the sound of footsteps, one set, leisurely in pace but even and certain in stride. Footsteps coming for him.

He doubted it was his miracle.

John squinted his good eye shut as the lightbulb snapped on and its harsh brightness seared his brain.

By the time he'd blinked his waiting visitor into focus, he finally understood why he'd been brought here. He looked into the eyes of an old friend. Resurrected from the past. John had wondered when keeping secrets would finally come back to bite him in the ass. Tonight was the night, apparently. "You."

"Me." The visitor was alone. Unapologetic. Unmoved by John's disfiguring injuries. "I see my men have been a little rough with you."

Bone-Crusher and Jaw-Smasher weren't too stupid to know when to back away from a threat like this one. They were long gone. Had they completed their task and been paid off and sent on their way? This one had never liked loose ends. If the two goons were still alive, that meant they were needed for some other purpose. Another job. More people hurt. Maybe even John's own family. His beautiful wife or one of his sons. "I thought you were dead."

"Not so much."

John had neither the strength nor the inclination to laugh. "I wrote about us. And what we did."

"A memoir. How touching. Those pages will never see the light of day, not unless you break your sworn oath—and all-American good guy that you are, I know you won't." His old *friend* moved closer, braced one arm against the arm of John's chair and leaned in. The fire in the voice was the same, the chill in the eyes unfazed by so many years apart. "What we *did*…was make a difference in the world. You. Me. All the others. We were visionaries."

John sat up as straight as his body would let him. "I never liked your vision of the future."

"You won't like yours now, either." His visitor stepped back, smiling. It was a cold imitation of humor. This smile was deadly.

So was the gun pointed at John's heart. "Goodbye, John."

Chapter One

Sawyer Kincaid hated the rain.

He hated the sound of it beating against the green canvas tent top. He resented the clingy mist of it masking the tears on his mother's pale cheeks, as though it could somehow wash away her grief. He loathed the spring-time chill of it running down the back of his neck beneath his collar.

But mostly he hated the way it beaded atop the black stripe that bisected the nickel-and-brass badge he wore on his chest—the way the moisture attached itself to every KCPD badge here.

Of course, he could move closer to the somber ceremony instead of standing back at the fringe of family and friends and colleagues. He could get under the tent, get out of the rain. But he was just too big a man to be standing at the front of the crowd if anyone else behind him wanted to see. Besides, getting closer wouldn't make the rain stop.

Getting closer wouldn't make the pain go away, either.

"…but come ye back when summer's in the meadow, or when the valley's hushed and white with snow…"

For a moment Sawyer tore his attention away from the rain's gloomy rhythm to listen to his youngest brother Holden's rich, melodic voice. Their father would have loved his a cappella rendition of "Danny Boy."

But how the twenty-eight-year-old *baby* of the Kincaid family could sing at a time like this was beyond Sawyer's understanding. Maybe the kid was more put together than he'd given him credit for. Sawyer could barely push the thank-yous and glad-you-cames and Dad-would-be-pleased-to-see-you-heres beyond the tight constriction of his throat. A neck as thick as his wasn't built for wearing button-down shirts and black silk ties. The last time he'd worn his police dress uniform had been when he'd received his detective's shield. His dad had been there that day, too, shaking his hand and beaming proudly.

Today, Thomas Sawyer Kincaid was burying his father in the ground.

In the damn rain.

This ain't right.

The nagging mantra had plagued him since that phone call from the commissioner five days ago. *"Your father's dead, Detective. John was murdered. His body was found in Swope Park—though the lab says that isn't the primary crime scene. I assure you, we're giving this case top priority. John was a good man. A good cop. He was my good friend. If there's anything I can do for any of you, let me know. I'm so sorry."*

Sawyer spotted the lady commissioner standing at the front of the crowd, waiting to say a few words about her colleague and friend. Commissioner Shauna Cartwright-Masterson had been a real class act about the whole thing—paying a couple of visits to his mother, Susan, and steering the press away from the family. But the commissioner could talk until she was blue in the face. There just weren't enough good words that anyone could say to make this right.

John Kincaid had survived walking a beat in downtown K.C. He'd survived being a detective in vice and homicide. Last year he'd led an organized-crime task force that had brought down the Wolfe International crime syndicate.

He should have survived a damn run in the park.

Sawyer shrugged the dampness and injustice of it all off his big shoulders, and concentrated on staying in the moment. He had to focus on the now, not the past, not the future—or else he'd start cussing or blubbering like a baby. An emotional outburst like that in front of all these people would be a real tribute to his father.

Like hell it would.

He blinked the stinging wetness from his eyes and inhaled a deep breath to cool his lungs. He turned away from troublesome thoughts and emotions and visually sought out the rest of his family.

Holden was wearing his dress blues, too. Standing at the foot of their father's flag-draped casket, he finished his song, saluted John Kincaid's memory, then resumed his seat beside their mother in the front row of chairs.

Another brother, Atticus, was in uniform as well, as he sat on the opposite side of Susan Kincaid with a stoic, unreadable look behind his dark-rimmed glasses. Atticus was the cool, calm and collected one. Though they'd all been spending time at the house these past few days, Atticus could keep it together better than any of them and provide the rock of support their mother would need.

The soil squished beneath Sawyer's size thirteens as he subtly shifted his stance to locate his oldest brother in the crowd of mourners. There, even farther from the main gathering than Sawyer, unshaven and scowling, leaning on his cane beneath an overhang of dripping pine boughs, stood thirty-five-year-old Edward Rochester Kincaid. Though he'd made lieutenant more than two years ago, Edward had refused to wear his uniform today. He'd reminded their mother that he was on disability leave from the force and wearing it would be awkward with all the veteran and active-duty officers in attendance. But Sawyer knew better. His mother knew better. *Awkward* didn't begin to describe what Edward must be feeling with all these people around. At a funeral. He hadn't just been out of touch with the department since the tragic attack that had robbed him of so much. He'd been out of touch with his friends and family. Out of touch with life. The fact that he'd shown up at all was a concession to Susan Kincaid's grief, and a nod of respect to their father.

But they were all here—Edward, Sawyer, Atticus and Holden. John Kincaid's four sons. Bonded by brotherhood. Forged into men by the badges they wore. Reunited by grief.

Knowledge of those family ties eased the constriction in his chest and Sawyer inhaled a deep, grounding breath.

"It isn't easy, is it."

Sawyer clenched his fists at his sides to mask his startled reaction to the voice beside him. He could do this. If his grieving mother could make nice with well-meaning friends who wanted to offer comfort and sympathy, and maybe find a little for themselves, then so could he. He angled his head toward a black umbrella and the distinguished gentleman who'd come up beside him. "No." *This sucks.* Nah, Mom wouldn't like him to say that here—even to an old family friend. He swallowed the emotion that seemed to paralyze his throat. "It's not."

There. He got some words out. Decent ones, too.

"Hang in there, son." William Caldwell reached up to squeeze Sawyer's shoulder. He wore his black suit with the same impeccable style as the gray streaking his temples. But underneath the businessman's facade, Sawyer knew there lurked a man who was more fraternity brother and army buddy to John Kincaid than wealthy entrepreneur and owner of his own computer technology company. "These are tough times. It's the second funeral for a friend I've been to since the beginning of the year. Your dad and I should be gearing up for retirement. Enjoying ourselves. It shouldn't end like this."

Sawyer and his brothers had gone hunting or fishing with Bill Caldwell and their dad more times than he could remember. They'd shared crazy stories over campfires. He'd absorbed words of wisdom from the old pros about catching fish and tracking game, talking to girls and living life like a man.

But Sawyer still wasn't ready to hear the speeches. He wasn't ready to join in the prayers. He wasn't ready to talk about the injustice that burned him right down to his soul.

Probably sensing the tenuous control Sawyer held on his civil demeanor, Caldwell patted his arm and pulled away. "You take care now."

Take care of what? Sawyer planed his hand down his face to clear the rain from his eyes and mouth. He needed to be doing something. He needed to move, to go. His palms were itching with the need to grab somebody by the throat and make them pay.

Even John Kincaid's easygoing, good-ol'-boy son had a temper inside him. And it was brewing. The emotions would boil over if he didn't do something about this travesty soon.

So there on the spot, standing in the rain, he gave himself a job to do.

There were plenty of folks here, honoring his father. Missing him. But amongst the honor guards, police and government officials, extended family and friends like Caldwell, Sawyer concentrated on something more important than tamping down his sorrow or anger.

He studied each face huddled inside the tent, standing beneath umbrellas and taking shelter under the green, soggy branches of the towering oaks and ash trees and pines lining the road that twisted through the hills of Kansas City's Mount Washington Cemetery. But he wasn't looking for familiar friends or comfort.

Sawyer was looking for a face that didn't fit. He was looking for someone watching the gathering and admiring the success of his handiwork—someone whose curiosity might be bolder than his brains. A smile of satisfaction amongst all the sorrow. He was looking for the man who'd beaten his father bloody and fired a bullet into his chest.

He was looking for his father's killer.

"Is this a joke?"

Sawyer switched the phone to his left ear and paced to the opposite end of the large country kitchen. Staring out the window over the sink into the blackness of the backyard he'd grown up in, he jerked the knot loose on his tie and unhooked the top two buttons of his soggy white shirt.

Finally, he had something useful to do to take his mind off the funeral and the friends and family who'd come to his mother's house afterward. But he'd trade almost anything for a different assignment.

"I wish. All three of them have vanished. Including our pal Longbow." Friend and fellow cop Detective Seth Cartwright, the commissioner's son, hadn't shown up for the potluck dinner after leaving the cemetery. Now Sawyer understood why. A nightmare from the organized-crime investigation they'd worked together last year had reawakened.

"He's no friend of mine."

"Mine, either. I know what that bastard can do." Like try to murder Seth's wife.

Sawyer knew Ace Longbow as a hulking, temperamental enforcer for the mob. In exchange for testifying against his former boss, he'd been given the opportunity to spend the rest of his life rotting away in prison, instead of facing a lethal injection himself. But something had gone very, very wrong at a courthouse in Jefferson City, Missouri, that afternoon. "You're sure he didn't die in the crash?"

They should be so lucky.

Seth continued. "We're listing all three as escaped prisoners until we've got bodies to confirm their deaths."

Sawyer scrubbed at the evening beard peppering his jaw. "What happened?"

"The Department Of Corrections in Jefferson City had him out to testify in the Wolfe case, along with two other prisoners who were involved in different federal investigations. From what I understand, there were weapons planted in the courtroom. Artillery fire from a van outside knocked out one of the walls."

"Artillery fire? Sounds like an invasion. Or terrorists."

"Somebody had some money and connections behind the escape. One prison escort is dead and another critical. At least three other personnel from the courthouse are hospitalized in serious condition. I don't know how many others suffered minor injuries. They kidnapped the stenographer, but dumped her before their getaway car went into the river. The feds are already on-site, along with the DOC and local authorities. They're still cleaning up the mess. State police claim at least one of the prisoners was hit before they rammed the car and knocked it off the bridge. They're dredging the river where the car went in, but have come up with nothing."

"Three escapees and at least one accomplice if those guns were planted, but no bodies have been found?" Sawyer didn't know whether to curse or laugh.

"Not one. No John Doe gunshot victims reported at any local hospitals. No one washed up on the banks. The Missouri has a deep channel and strong currents in that part of the state, so they could be miles downstream by now. Longbow and the others could be anywhere in Missouri, anywhere in the country by now. Hell, if he survived, he could be back here in K.C."

Sawyer's muscles jumped with the desire to join in the manhunt. But pacing off the length of the kitchen seemed to be his only option right now. "And there are no leads?"

Seth's no was colorful and emphatic. "It's no secret that Longbow's former boss, Theodore Wolfe, took out a hit on Longbow—to shut his mouth and keep Ace from testifying against him. As easy as it is to off a guy in lockup, why go to all this trouble? Besides, we shut Wolfe down—turned over all his men to Interpol or local authorities. If he still has the connections to pull off something this big, then he'd have left the body to prove it."

Seth had survived turning on the Wolfes himself. Saywer's father had survived bringing the Wolfe family to justice. Was John Kincaid's murder related to Longbow's escape from prison?

"I thought you should know," Seth went on, explaining the real purpose behind this call on this day. "You were there at the casino to provide backup for me while I was under-cover with the Wolfe family, and I know you developed some kind of…attachment to Longbow's ex-wife."

The pacing stopped.

Melissa Teague. Single mom and cocktail

waitress. Sawyer had been playing bartender and bouncer back then and had worked with Melissa. An image of her small, perfectly proportioned figure filling out that skimpy saloon-girl costume the waitresses had worn popped into his mind, as vivid and distracting as the real woman had been. He remembered Melissa as a pretty little slip of a thing—all blue eyes and golden hair. And bruises. Sprained wrists.

And fear.

"We all wanted to take care of her." But they had all failed her.

The sandwich Sawyer had wolfed down to appease his mother churned in his stomach at the memory of seeing Melissa in a hospital bed, looking small and pale as she lay in a coma, fighting for her life. The last time he'd seen her awake, she'd rolled over in the hospital bed and turned her back on him. Even though he'd told her he'd been working undercover, that he was a cop and the bartender she'd known as Tom Sawyer was really Thomas Sawyer Kincaid, she still associated him with the Wolfe crime family and the place where Ace Longbow had tried to kill her.

Or maybe an oversize, overbuilt truck of a

man lurking in her doorway was too much of a reminder of her abusive ex.

Sawyer hissed a frustrated breath through tightly clenched teeth. He had no special claim on Melissa. She'd made it clear that, despite sharing a few cups of coffee before work, or walking her to her car after closing, she wanted nothing to do with him. Maybe not with any man. Considering her background, he couldn't blame her. "Why call me?"

"So far, we've been able to keep the escapees' names out of the press and the details sketchy. We've got every man on this. As soon as we got the wire from Jeff City, we dispatched a car to Melissa's house to keep an eye on things." Seth's long pause bespoke the depth of the favor he was asking of Sawyer. "I know the timing sucks. But I figured she'd rather hear the news from a familiar face than a stranger."

"Ah, hell." He finally had it fixed in his brain that he'd never see Melissa again. That was the only way he'd been able to get past the guilt and the wanting.

"Can you handle it tonight? If not, I'll take a break and go over there myself. She should know that her ex-husband escaped, and that he's either dead or missing."

Sawyer had been a cop for ten years. He'd been John Kincaid's son long before that. Doing the hard thing—doing the right thing—simply because it had to be done wasn't something he'd backed down from before. He wouldn't skip out on his duty now. No matter how raw he was already feeling inside. "No. You know the players better than any of us. You need to be there at the precinct office to keep track of information as it comes in. I'll go."

"Thanks, Sawyer." Seth apologized for his and his wife's early departure after the funeral. "I'm sorry Bec and I didn't make it to the reception. You know how much John meant to both of us. But when the call came in—"

"Forget it. I'm glad you're there to handle it."

"I had a lot of respect for your dad."

"We all did." The heartfelt words should have calmed him, centered him. But for a man who was used to doing rather than talking, the lengthy conversation made him antsy to get this errand over with. "You go back to work. I'll get over to Melissa's."

Seth seemed to understand, and traded instructions instead of goodbyes. "Flash your badge to the man in the squad car.

Captain Taylor gave him orders to shoot first and ask questions later if anyone approaches the house."

"Got it."

"Is there a problem, son?" The swinging kitchen door closed behind Susan Kincaid as Sawyer hung up the phone. She looked tired, like she wasn't eating enough, like maybe there were a few more threads of gray in her dark brown hair than had been there a week ago.

But Sawyer still stood up a little straighter when she crossed her arms and tilted her chin with that I-dare-you-to-lie-to-me look that had gotten him to fess up from the time he was a small boy. "I'm sorry. Something's come up at work. I need to go take care of it."

That stern-mama look had never lasted for long. It didn't now. Instead, Susan reached up and tugged Sawyer's wrinkled tie free from his collar. She smoothed the front of his unbuttoned uniform jacket and straightened his shirt. "Of all my boys, you never were one to sit still and worry things through for very long. Probably why you were the one we always had to drive to the emergency room." Her hands settled at the center of his chest, warming Sawyer all the way through to his heart.

"Staying dressed up and putting on a game face all day long must be driving you crazy."

Sawyer grinned. "You think you know me that well, huh?"

"Please. After thirty-two years, I know you better than you know yourself. If you need to crash out and take care of something, do it. Your father's assistant, Brooke, is here to help me, and she's keeping things running so efficiently that there's nothing much for any of us to do. Your brothers will understand if you need to leave. I understand." She turned him toward door and gave him a push. "Now go. Just give me a call later so I know you're all right."

Though Susan Kincaid's will was a force to be reckoned with, Sawyer was twice her size and refused to be ushered out just yet. He turned at the door, scooped her up in a bear hug and planted a kiss on her cheek before setting her down. "I love you, Mom."

She smiled. It was the first real smile he'd seen on her throughout this long, long day. "I know."

Chapter Two

Twenty-five minutes later, Sawyer pulled his truck up behind the black and white, killed the lights and wipers and turned off the engine. A smile from his mom had improved his mood if not his trepidation about tonight's visit to Melissa Teague's tiny white house in the Kansas City suburb of Independence. The place was neat, but plain and unassuming, showing the signs of its age in the sag of the front porch and the cracks running through the brickwork along the house's foundation.

He pulled his badge from his jacket and slipped it back into his wallet before checking the gun on his belt and climbing out. Squinting into the rain, he braced his shoulders for the unpleasant task at hand and moved toward the officer in the squad car.

"I'm a friend of the family," he explained,

fudging a little on the *friend* part as the blue suit read his badge and ID and okayed him to approach the house.

Sawyer caught a glimpse of his drowned-rat reflection when the officer rolled up his window against the moisture splashing into his car. Big scary man coming in from the dark and the storm. Yeah, he'd be a real reassuring sight.

One more reason to hate the rain.

Muttering a curse that was half damnation, half resignation to the inevitable, Sawyer jumped the torrent running along the curb and hurried across the street. Pausing for a quick scan up and down the sidewalk and into the side yards, he made sure there were no unwelcome eyes watching the place. In fact, other than the officer in the car, the block was deserted. The isolation of locked doors and dark windows nagged at him almost as much as the sight of someone spying on the house would have. But he supposed he was the only one without the sense to stay in on a night like this. Tomorrow, he'd order a rundown on all the neighbors to make sure there were no empty houses and that the residents were who they said they were.

Resolved that he could at least do that much to keep Melissa safe, Sawyer climbed the steps onto her front porch. The wood shifted and creaked beneath his weight, groaning like an ominous portent of unseen danger. But the light beside the door was on, so she'd be able to get a good look at him before opening it.

He pressed the doorbell, then shook the excess water from his unbuttoned jacket, making sure his Glock was tucked out of sight behind his back. He was squeegeeing the rain from his hair when the inside door nudged open a crack.

Sawyer braced for the impact of seeing Melissa again.

But the breath he'd been holding eased from his chest in an odd mixture of disappointment and relief as he caught his first glimpse of the woman peeking over the chain latching the door to its frame.

Not Melissa. Just as petite, though, maybe five foot two or three at the most. Pretty in a soft sort of feminine way that must be an inherited trait. The wary suspicion in this woman's eyes was similar. But the hair was shorter, curlier, laced with silver amongst the gold. "Yes?"

"Mrs. Teague?"

"Who's asking?"

Sawyer held his badge up beside his face. "KCPD, ma'am. I'm Detective Kincaid from the Fourth Precinct."

The older woman squinted. "The Fourth Precinct's in downtown Kansas City. What are you doing out…? Oh, shoot." She turned away from the door and shouted inside. "Benjamin? Bring Grandma her glasses. Please." She looked back through the screen that separated her from Sawyer. "I wondered when someone was going to come up to the house. That police car has been sitting out there for a half hour. I was still cleaning the dinner dishes when he pulled up. Makes me nervous."

"It's just a precaution, ma'am. He's keeping an eye on the neighborhood." Sawyer tucked his badge onto his belt and retreated a step to hopefully ease her concern. "Is Miss Teague here?"

"Gandma?" Short, chubby fingers pushed a pair of glasses into the woman's hands, and then a little boy with shaggy black hair, barefoot and dressed in overalls, peeked around her leg.

Sawyer's pulse hitched in recognition as

he looked down into a carbon copy of Melissa's clear blue eyes.

"Hey, pal. How's it goin'?" Sawyer grinned at the little guy. He must be three years old. He barely cleared Sawyer's knee, but there was no mistaking the bold curiosity in his expression as he inched his way around his grandmother's leg and craned his neck to look up into Sawyer's face.

"I can't talk to stwangers," he announced very wisely.

Sawyer nudged the boy's age up to four, or maybe twelve or thirty-six, judging by his verbal abilities. "That's smart." He held out his ID again, now that the woman at the door had her glasses on. "Did your mom teach you that?"

"How come you're so big?"

Laughter was the only option with a question like that. "*My* mom's a good cook. And I'm a good eater."

"I'm a good eater, too."

"Of course." The woman snapped her fingers in recognition, drawing Sawyer's focus back up. "You're that man who came to visit Melissa in the hospital. The co-worker from when she was waitressing at the Riverboat Casino. I don't know that she was ever awake while you were there. For a long time, I didn't think she was going to come out of that coma. I'm Fritzi Teague, Melissa's mother. This is her son, Benjamin." Her welcoming chatter slowed into suspicion once more. "I thought she said you were a bartender, though."

"That's how she knew me at the time. But I was working a case. I assure you I'm a cop." He wondered if he should offer to let her call in his badge number for verification. "It's a long story. Is Melissa here?"

"She's at her accounting class tonight. She usually gets home around nine-thirty." Fritzi hugged little Benjamin closer to her leg and dropped her voice to a whisper. "Is something wrong? Has something happened to her?"

"No, ma'am," Sawyer quickly reassured her. "I wouldn't be asking for her here if I thought she'd been hurt in any way." Logical words in almost any case. Still, a tremor of uneasy awareness rippled over his shoulders at the idea that Ace Longbow had somehow survived his bloody escape and had already found a way to get to the Kansas City area and track down his ex-wife. "I'd like to wait and speak to her in person if I could."

The older woman's gaze darted down to

her grandson. She offered Sawyer an apologetic smile when she looked back up. "My daughter doesn't like anyone to come inside when she's not here. Especially at night."

Sawyer glanced over his shoulder at the steady curtain of rain whipping ahead of the wind. A soft drumbeat of thunder mocked him in the distance. But even as he shifted inside his soggy clothes, he had to admire the Teague women's efforts to keep their little family safe. "No problem, ma'am. I'll be out in my truck."

"Wait." Fritzi called him back from the edge of the porch. "It's not like you're a complete stranger. And since you're the police, well, I just made a pot of decaf coffee. I don't suppose it could hurt if you came inside and warmed yourself up. Just let me get the door."

As she closed the door to unlatch the chain, Sawyer made a mental note to ensure there were secure locks on every entrance to the house. If Fritzi Teague thought that flimsy chain would keep unwelcome visitors out, she was living with a false sense of security. He hated to tell Melissa's mother that he could have cut through the screen and busted down the door with little more than a shove.

If she didn't keep the dead bolt fastened, the chain and the knob lock would barely slow him down, much less stop him if he wanted to get inside. And they sure as hell wouldn't stop a fanatic like Ace Longbow.

Sawyer fixed a smile on his mouth and, for the moment, kept his concerns to himself when she reopened the door and invited him inside.

MELISSA TEAGUE SPOTTED the black-and-white police cruiser parked in front of her house the moment she turned her old Pontiac around the corner.

The ingrained alertness that had become as much a part of her as breathing kicked up to warning levels, speeding her pulse and sharpening her senses. She squeezed the steering wheel in her fists and pressed a little harder on the gas.

She didn't recognize the black truck, either.

Melissa splashed through the lake pooling at the end of her driveway and parked her car up beside the house. She left the bag of groceries tipped over in the passenger seat, grabbed her keys and climbed out into the rain.

"Mom?" She turned up the collar of her

trench coat, blinked the beads of moisture from her eyelashes and spared a glance for the officer in his car. Drinking his coffee. Just sitting. He wasn't on his radio or writing up a report as though the truck was illegally parked or stolen, or if there'd been a break-in. Still, surprises had never been a good thing for her. Especially this close to home. "Benjamin?"

Forcing her lungs to breathe deeply and evenly, she ran across the slick grass to the porch. She quickly unlocked the knob and dead bolt, cursed when she discovered the chain wasn't fastened and pushed her way inside. "Mom!"

The screen door slammed shut behind her as she hurried toward the light streaming through the archway from the living room. "Ben? Mom? Why won't you answer—"

She turned the corner and froze.

Her mother was sitting on the sofa, cradling a coffee mug between her hands and laughing with rare abandon—laughing at the man wrestling with Melissa's precious son on the braided rug.

For one awful moment she thought that Ace… But no, Benjamin might be a dead ringer for his father with his black hair and olive skin, but her ex had never claimed him. He'd seen their child as a threat—as competition for her love. To Ace, their son was an abomination. A betrayal. Ace had never accepted any other males in her life—not even his own child.

All the more reason to hold her little boy close and keep him safe.

The man's deep voice cracked as he teased Benjamin with a high-pitched plea for mercy. "Aagh! Big Ben got me!"

"Get *me*! Get *me*!"

"You asked for it." Her four-year-old squealed in delight as the dark-haired man closed him in a scissor hold between his knees and rolled back and forth on the floor.

You asked for it. Melissa blocked out the painful memory the words conjured and found her voice. "Mother!"

The wrestling ceased in an instant. Her mother's smile vanished. "Melissa."

"Mommy!" Benjamin beamed from one flushed cheek to the other. "'Tective got me!"

Melissa gripped the door frame and retreated half a step as the man sat up and scooted Benjamin onto his lap.

Oh my God.

She wasn't ready for a reunion like this.

"Hey." The slightly breathless laugh that lingered in their guest's bass voice should have reassured her with its familiarity. His lazy grin should have struck a pang of welcome recognition instead of tensing every muscle with the urge to turn and run from the remembered horrors of her old life.

Melissa Teague didn't run anymore. But standing her ground still didn't come easy.

She knew this man. Not exactly a stranger. Not exactly an old friend, either. His straight, coffee-brown hair was shorter than she re-membered, his clothes certainly different. Tom Sawyer. No, that wasn't right. Tom Sawyer Kincaid. He'd said something about his mom being an English teacher who'd named all her sons after characters in books. He'd said something about being a cop— something about asking her out and getting to know her better.

"What are you doing here?" was the only greeting that worked its way past the guarded tension squeezing her throat.

"Melissa—your manners!" her mother chided, setting down her coffee and rising to her feet.

As her initial panic ebbed, an embarrass-ing self-consciousness took its place. He was looking at her in *that* way. The way a man who wanted something looked at a woman.

Before she was completely aware of doing it, Melissa combed her fingers through the hair at her left temple, urging a golden wave over her cheek. But just as quickly, hating even that revelation of weakness about herself, she squared her shoulders and marched across the room to pluck her son from the officer's arms. "Benjamin's too small for roughhousing with you."

"Mommy, you're wet. I want down."

"I didn't hurt him. Boys like to wrestle—"

"Get me again!" Benjamin reached for their guest.

"See?"

The man's lopsided grin was just as innocently boyish as her son's. In another lifetime, she might have succumbed to its charm.

But this was the life she had to deal with. Despite Benjamin's squiggles to climb down and resume the game, she wedged him firmly on her hip. "Why is there a police car parked in front of my house?"

"I let Detective Kincaid in, dear," her mother explained. "He's only been here a half hour or so. I checked his ID before opening the door. Don't you remember him?"

"Of course I remember—"

"Better let me handle this." The man she'd known as Tom Sawyer, a bartender with a sweet but misplaced sense of responsibility for the waitresses who worked with him, smoothed the scattered strands of hair off his forehead and rolled to his feet. He stood. And stood. Melissa's pulse quickened with an instinctive self-preservation and she backed away.

His warm brown gaze darted to the subtle movement of her feet. But she didn't apologize or make excuses.

He didn't ask for any. "It's good to see you again, Mel."

She forced her gaze up past the evening beard that studded his square jaw, and acknowledged his greeting with a nod. "Tom."

He raised his focus and skimmed her face, probably noting the newer, shoulder-length cut of her hair—probably satisfying his curiosity about how her injuries had healed as well. "You look great."

He looked…male.

Ignoring the little tremor of awareness that blipped through her brain, Melissa concentrated on all the reasons why she'd never picked up a phone to resume their friendship, never encouraged him to turn that friendship into something more. One, he was an old-fashioned kind of guy—the sort who held open doors, sent flowers and who'd try to make everything right for her. Two, nice as he'd seemed back at the casino where they'd worked together, he'd lied about who he was. What he did for a living. Why he'd been so interested in her. And whether or not the lie was unavoidable and he really was one of the good guys, she couldn't afford to be fooled by good intentions and false promises. She couldn't allow herself to drop her guard and be taken in by any man—even a nice one. Especially a nice one. She needed her independence in order to survive.

And three? *Oh, hell.* She remembered thinking Tom Sawyer Kincaid might be the one man in her life with the brawn and bravado to stand up to her ex-husband. The man who'd come galloping to her rescue. But any chivalrous fantasy she might have toyed with scared the hell out of her, too. She'd forgotten just how imposing he could be, with those broad shoulders and thick forearms, every sinew and hollow made blatantly evident by the sticky second skin of his damp white shirt and rolled-up sleeves.

She couldn't help but compare. There'd been so many times she wished she'd met a man like Detective Kincaid before Ace had ever walked into her sheltered life back in South Dakota. But wishing didn't help reality. There were no more fantasies to be dreamed, no trust to be given. There was only survival.

So she sloughed off his compliment and ignored the spark of interest her female instincts tried to rouse in her. "I look worn-out from a day that's gone on way too long."

"It's been a long one for me, too." He splayed his fingers at his hips, drawing attention to the badge with the black stripe bisecting it that was clipped to his belt. Did that black stripe have anything to do with this surprise visit?

"More 'Get me!'" Benjamin pushed against Melissa's chest, saving her from the compassionate impulse to ask about that black stripe and the length of his day.

"Not now, sweetie. It's getting late." She stroked his silky black hair and hugged him a little tighter, to settle her own nerves as much as his. But she kept her eyes on their guest. She needed a safer topic. "What's it been? A year?"

"Not quite. I haven't seen you since last July."

Not so safe.

Last July she'd been in the hospital, broken and unconscious. Even now, the events that had put her in that ICU bed were hazy. But she remembered his last visit. Though she couldn't recall his words, she remembered being just as frightened as she'd been pleased to see him. He'd asked for something from her, something she couldn't—wouldn't—give to a man again.

Her affection? Her trust? Permission to give those things to her? Was that why he was here tonight? Did he think enough time had passed—could *ever* pass—for her to give a new relationship a chance?

"So what are you doing here?" she asked again.

He reached for a dark blue uniform jacket draped over the back of a chair, and picked up a holstered gun he'd set high up on the mantel of her fake fireplace. He'd come here armed? With another officer sitting outside? This visit wasn't personal, after all.

"Can we talk? Someplace private?"

Even if that grin had stayed in place, she would have suspected his motives for showing up at her home unannounced.

After a slight hesitation, she nodded. Giving him a wide berth as she circled around him, Melissa handed Ben off to her mother, trading a reassuring hug with the older woman and giving her son a kiss. "Benjamin needs to be getting to bed. Do you mind starting his bath?"

"Of course not. Thanks for the company, Mr. Kincaid."

"I appreciate the coffee, ma'am."

Benjamin stretched out both arms toward his new playmate and curled his fingers into a wave. "Bye, 'tective."

"See ya, Big Ben."

Her mother reached out and squeezed her hand. "Honey, Mr. Kincaid isn't the enemy." Melissa weathered a sad, maybe even apologetic, frown, then turned away as Fritzi carried her grandson down the hallway toward the bathroom at the back of the house.

"We can talk in the kitchen, Tom."

He followed her across the hallway to the room where she could turn on the brightest lights and put a solid piece of furniture, namely the width of her kitchen table, between them. "Thomas is my first name, but I go by Sawyer in real life."

Real life. Ha. She'd been crazy to worry

for even one moment about him seeing the changes in her appearance after a shattered face and reconstructive surgeries. Her reality didn't include old friends stopping by for let's-get-reacquainted visits. Her reality included living paycheck to paycheck, working when she wasn't going to school, updating restraining orders and looking over her shoulder.

She flipped on the overhead light switch beside the door and crossed to the sink to turn on the light there, too. But the bright lights and distance between them did little to diminish his overpowering presence. The smells of earthy dampness clinging to their clothes and skin intensified in the smaller room, giving the atmosphere an intimate electricity she shouldn't be feeling.

Attraction of any kind—emotional attachments beyond her mother and son—weren't an option for her. She needed to be on guard. Always. The last six years of her life had taught her that.

She unfastened the top two buttons of her raincoat and straightened her collar before crossing her arms in front of her and bracing herself for whatever he had to say. "Okay— Sawyer—does this have something to do with the Wolfes' illegal activities at the casino? When I gave my deposition at the hospital, the D.A. said he didn't think I'd have to testify in person."

"As far as I know, you won't." Watching him unhook his belt and strap his gun and holster back into place wasn't exactly reassuring. "To my knowledge, the case against Theodore Wolfe is still tight. Once the state of Missouri is done with him, he'll be taken back to London to face international charges."

"Then what's wrong? Why are you here?"

"It's your husband. Ace Longbow."

"My *ex*-husband," she corrected. The handsome man who'd first beaten her the night he'd accused her of getting pregnant to trap him into marriage. The flowers and apologies and diamond ring he'd brought her the next day had fooled her. Ace Longbow, the exciting, slightly dangerous man, who—as a nineteen-year-old barely out of high school— she'd naively thought she could tame.

She'd mistaken passion for love. Control for caring.

She'd thought a divorce would end the torture.

But the man who, to this day, claimed to love her in the letters that went straight to her attorney, had accused her of betraying his loyalty to the Wolfe crime family and had dragged her down to the river to kill her.

Melissa self-consciously touched the scar on her cheek, then quickly turned away to busy her hands with pouring herself a cup of coffee. The bones had mended. And the surgeons had done a good job of rebuilding her shattered face. But the scar they'd left behind was functional, not pretty. And until she could get ahead on her bills, a plastic surgeon was out of the question.

It wasn't vanity so much as the violence it represented that made her sensitive about the long, curving mark. Every time she washed her face or brushed her hair in the mirror, she saw the brand of her shameful marriage stamped there. "What about Ace? Has something happened to him?"

"I'm sorry. I guess you haven't seen the news this evening."

News? Sawyer's shadow fell over her, consuming her breathing space. The coffeepot rattled against her cup. He rescued the objects from her shaking grasp and set them safely on the counter. But the surprising gentleness of even that impersonal touch chilled her to the bone.

This couldn't be good.

Melissa curled her fingers into her palms and scooted some distance between them, steeling herself for the worst. With Richard "Ace" Longbow, there was always a *worst*. "Sorry about what?"

"He escaped with two other inmates from a courthouse in Jefferson City this afternoon. Authorities there believe he was shot. The getaway car they were in ran off the bridge and plunged into the Missouri River."

The words swam inside her head. She gripped the edge of the counter to stop the dizzying sensation. "Are you telling me Ace is dead?"

Sawyer's silence lasted a beat too long. Her world instantly righted itself with cold, numbing clarity. She angled her gaze up to Sawyer's eyes. "You don't know if he's alive or dead. You don't know where he is."

His big shoulders lifted, absorbing the weight of the accusation. "Since none of the bodies have turned up, we're assuming all three fugitives are still alive. But they've gone underground and disappeared. We don't know where Ace is or what his plans might entail. But we're doing everything we can to find him."

Melissa didn't bother asking where

Sawyer and the prison authorities thought Ace might be headed. If Ace wasn't dead, there was only one answer.

Here.

Chapter Three

"Ace? Ace?"

Timid hands brushed his face and nudged at his shoulder.

"C'mon, big guy. Wake up."

Melissa Teague's voice was as soothing as her gentle touch. Growing up the bastard son of Lionel Pritchard, and raised by his whoring mistress on the reservation where everyone knew his shame, Ace Longbow had never known gentleness in his life. But this white girl, this shy little wacicu from the high school in town where he'd gone to get a man's job, treated him like he was something fragile. Something good. She talked to him like he was more wind than ox. Like she cared. Like she belonged to him.

"I can feel you breathing, so I know you're not dead." Her gentle hands cupped his *cheek. "But you are scaring me. Those idiots are gone now. Please."*

A grin teased his bloodied mouth as his brain slowed its spinning and his senses began to return. "I'm not dead, little one," he slurred around his split lip.

Was that a relieved sob on his behalf? His grin widened and pain speared through his jaw. He forced the automatic clench of muscles to relax, knowing that was the only way to work through the ache of the hits he'd taken. But his weary groan earned him another touch—fingers brushing back the hair at his temple. An intimate touch.

"Thank goodness. You're my hero. Now please open your eyes so I know you're okay."

Yeah. This one was worth taking on a trio of town boys over. Only people who didn't know him were stupid enough to pick a fight with him. And those three, teasing the girl at the Yankton Café nearly to tears had been nothin' but stupid. "I'm awake," he assured her, blinking open his eyes to look up into her pretty, concerned face. "You're safe now. Just hold me a little longer and I'll be all right."

She adjusted his head in her lap as she bent to press a kiss to his forehead. Savoring her tender affection, Ace's eyes drifted shut. She smelled so sweet. Talked so nice. Yeah, she might say they were just acquaintances because he came in to eat at the place where she worked. But things had changed for them tonight. They were more than acquaintances. More than friends. She was already his.

"M'lissa..." he moaned. Wished. Wanted.

"He's comin' around."

The deep male voice grated against Ace's eardrums, invading the memory that gave him such comfort. He grunted at the intrusive sound and tried to recapture the hazy dream.

"He better wake up. I'm not haulin' his ass out of any more rivers."

Time and memories began to merge. The linoleum floor at the Yankton Cafè became a cold concrete wall at his back. Melissa's soothing voice gave way to the familiar whine of the man who'd slept on the bunk above Ace for the last three days.

"Who hauled who out of the water, you little prick?" The deep voice again. "Now help me move this guy so I can tie off the bandage."

Ace was mildly aware of his sleeve being removed, his undershirt ripped off him. Rough hands roamed over his shoulder and chest. There was no gentleness in these touches.

"All right, all right. Ease up. You're the big man. I'm just the driver." Hank Brenner-man's voice whined close to his ear and Ace swatted at the sound as if it was a pesky gnat. He slumped forward, but Hank's buzzing continued. "Hank, do this. Ace, do that. I know you ain't got the connections to pull off what happened at that courthouse, Tyrell. Bribing a guard at county lockup to get us all on the same transport van. Planting a gun in the courtroom. The big guns outside. I tell ya, when that stone wall caved in, it was like freakin' D-day—"

A big hand pressed directly against Ace's wound, igniting a flash fire that seared through his shoulder. He came up swinging. "Get off me!"

Fully awake and raging at the pain radiating down his arm and up into his neck, Ace calmed his breathing and squinted Tyrell Mayweather into focus. The black man rubbed the blood away from the corner of his mouth as he pushed himself up from the floor where Ace had laid him out. "All right, chief. You get *one*. Just because you were out of it for a while and maybe didn't know what you were doin'." He held up one finger as a warning. "Just one."

Right. Like Mayweather was the biggest threat he had to worry about when there was a price on his head.

While Tyrell crawled to his feet and Hank wisely kept his distance, Ace took stock of his injuries and tried to remember everything that had happened over the last twelve hours. Grabbing the evidence gun that was loaded "by mistake." Shooting the first guard. Climbing through the broken wall beside Tyrell and diving into the car behind Hank. He'd taken a bullet to the shoulder and had hit his head on something in the river—or in the crash on the way down. The rest of it was fuzzy. Now they were here.

Ace sniffed at the shadows of the cavernous building and leaned back against the cinder-block wall. This place stunk like old raw meat and the dried river mud that stiffened the remnants of the orange jumpsuit he wore. It was as far away from the sweet smells of his dream as a man could get. "Where are we?" he demanded, looking to Hank, who had learned during their first meeting who was boss.

His jockey-size cell mate, with a knack for hacking computers and a tendency to mow down security guards who got in his way, didn't hesitate to answer. "We're at the place where Tyrell said we're supposed to meet his contact. About halfway to Kansas City, on an abandoned acreage inside somebody's old hog barn."

That explained the rancid smell. "What time is it?"

"Time for you to stop askin' questions, chief."

If Tyrell called him *chief* one more time… "Hank?"

"About midnight, Ace. Leastwise, last time I saw the clock in the car, that'd be about right."

"And you ditched the car so no one'll spot us here?"

Tyrell turned and advanced. "Hey! I'm runnin' this show. Trust me, I took care of everything. My friend will be here any minute."

Yeah, like he'd trust his life to a man who, up until two weeks ago when he'd approached Hank with the escape plan, had been part of a gang that was Ace's sworn enemy inside the pen. Funny how the opportunity for freedom could turn enemies into allies. But nobody had ever looked out for Ace but Ace. "So where is this so-called friend?"

"He'll be here."

"If you've set me up, I promise, you'll die before you leave this barn."

"Tough talk for a man with a bullet already in him, and a nice payout for the guy who finishes the job."

A familiar rage pumped through Ace's blood. A strong man never backed down from a challenge. Reaching behind him, he pulled the stolen gun from the back of his waistband and leveled the barrel at Tyrell. "I've still got a bullet left for you."

"Screw you." Tyrell charged. "I should've shanked you when—"

"Gentlemen."

Friend, my ass. The black man skidded to a halt so fast, he nearly toppled over. While Tyrell retreated a step, Ace slowly lowered the gun and assessed their visitors.

He recognized a boss when he saw one. This one might dress it up with a slick suit and turned-up nose at the stench of this place, but there was power there that owned the room and demanded respect—that demanded obeisance, at least. Following behind, a white-haired man with tats on his arms and colorless eyes did just that. Obey.

Without saying a word, he tossed a bundle to each of them and stepped back into place while the boss talked. "These are civilian clothes, prepaid cell phones and an envelope of cash and identification documents. I've arranged transportation for each of you as I want you to split up. As a group, you're too easy to track. I have different assignments for each of you, anyway, befitting your background and expertise. You'll find a weapon and sufficient ammunition in each of your vehicles."

"Who are you?" Ace asked.

"It's my job to know names and make things happen. It's your job to do what I say." The dark eyes narrowed. With suspicion? Disdain? That scornful look, suggesting Ace might not measure up, reminded him of Lionel Pritchard's easy dismissal of his existence. "Will you be able to fulfill your part of the bargain, Mr. Longbow?"

Ace braced his good arm on the wall behind him and curled his knees to stand. His shoulder burned with even that tiniest of exertions, but he hid the pain and stood tall. Like always. "I can do whatever job you give me."

"Good." The boss quickly lost interest in Ace's effort to prove himself. "I'd suggest getting some rest first. But by the end of seventy-two hours, I expect your tasks to be completed. Meanwhile, I'll plant enough false leads to keep the authorities off your trail. I'll contact each of you individually with your assignments."

"What if we can't get the job done in seventy-two hours?" Hank asked.

"That's not an option for you, Mr. Brennerman. I went to a lot of trouble and expense to get you out. I expect to be repaid."

"By workin' for you?"

The suit laughed. "A little slow on the uptake, aren't you, Mr. Brennerman."

"'Zat a slam?"

Ace might have laughed, too, if he was given to that sort of thing. He was more interested in the bargain being struck here. "We do this job and that's it? We don't owe you anything more?"

"Forget my face and that this meeting ever took place, of course. But yes, accomplish the task I give you, and we'll never have to see or speak to each other again." Long fingers brushed a smudge of dirt off a pinstriped sleeve. "Once you've served your purpose, you're free to live out your lives with anyone anywhere, in any way you wish. Though I would recommend a foreign country with no extradition standing."

Anyone. Anywhere.

"Good enough." Ace would take the job—not because he had a sense of honor and liked to repay what he owed, not because the money in that envelope was extremely generous and he could probably earn even more if he performed to the boss's satisfaction.

He took the job because he'd been given seventy-two hours on the outside.

He was free.

He was alive.

And in seventy-two hours, he could find Melissa.

"SCUBA GEAR."

Thunder rumbled outside the windows of the KCPD headquarters briefing room, giving a dramatic emphasis to the speaker's odd pronouncement. Sawyer set his empty coffee cup on the long, narrow table in front of him and leaned back in his chair as Special Agent Riley Holt of the FBI held up a plastic evidence bag. The bag contained a small air tank and mouthpiece, and explained a lot about how Ace Longbow and his prison buddies could disappear so completely once their car hit the Missouri River.

The FBI's poster boy for fast-track success might have earned the authority he wore as comfortably as that tailored suit of his, but there was something about the pressed tie and superior attitude that left Sawyer drumming his fingers on the arm of his chair in a subtle rebellion against the length of this interdepartmental briefing, and the protocol the feds were shoving down their throats.

Just give them the facts, tell them the plan and put them to work.

With a trio of killers on the loose, the Kincaid brothers weren't taking any chances. Sawyer and his brother Atticus had postponed the rest of their bereavement leave to report for duty, while their youngest brother, Holden, stayed with their mother to help sort through their father's things and to keep a watchful eye and supportive shoulder close by.

But they were here to work—to track down Longbow, Mayweather and Brennerman—not to sit and listen to a lecture on criminology procedures.

"This was as well-planned as any covert mission," Holt droned on, wasting more precious minutes while the line of rain that crossed the state from Saint Louis to K.C.

washed away any clues the three felons turned cop killers might have left behind. "Now, when my team recovered the Jackmon brothers out of Saint Louis, we found that..."

If it wasn't for the bleak resignation that had rendered Melissa's dewy skin an unnatural shade of pale last night when he'd told her of her ex's escape, Sawyer would have stayed away from KCPD headquarters altogether. He'd planned to use his time off to do some unofficial digging into his father's murder. He'd done his duty by Melissa and had prepared himself to walk away before those soulful blue eyes got under his skin and made him crazy with wanting her again. But there was no walking away now that he'd seen the tremulous resolve stamped in the determined set of her chin and shoulders.

Melissa expected the worst—from her ex, from life—maybe even from Sawyer himself. He supposed, with the history of violence she'd endured, he couldn't blame her. But Sawyer wasn't going to let her be disappointed again. At least, *he* wasn't going to be the one who failed her.

Whether she knew it or not, it was at that moment—in the middle of a dark, rainy night, while he was still railing against the injustice of his father's death—that Sawyer Kincaid became a part of Melissa Teague's life again.

The pink half moon of the scar on her face stood out like a badge of courage on her fair skin. And while every cell in him wanted to wrap her up in his arms and promise that he'd keep her safe, that he wouldn't let Ace and his obsessive, destructive hands get anywhere near her again, Melissa's cool *"Thank you for informing me. We'll be fine."* had kept him rooted in place.

That gutsy, maybe half-foolish assertion of independence had probably affected him more than if she *had* turned to him for comfort. He'd always known that what Melissa's slender body lacked in stature, she made up for in spirit. But standing straight and isolated in that kitchen tugged at something deep inside him. Standing there, hugging her arms around her waist and staring at her reflection in the window that separated them from the black, rain-filled night, made Sawyer think of the last man standing at the end of a battle. She had a mother and a child in her life, but in so many ways, she was more isolated than anyone he'd ever known.

And hell, nobody should be alone like that. Alone meant vulnerable.

Alone meant he was going to play backup. Even if she didn't want him as a friend, didn't want him in her house or playing with her kid, he'd still be there for her. He'd do his job as a cop and keep Ace out of her life. If nothing ever came of the longing for the single mom that had been simmering inside him for more than a year, it wouldn't matter. Melissa Teague would never be alone— or vulnerable—again. Not when he could do something about it.

But packed in a room with fifty other cops, representing every precinct in the Kansas City area, listening to Riley Holt lay out the chain of command in the interdepartmental task force he was spearheading, was feeling like a mighty big chunk of sitting around and doin' nothing. He got that the feds took priority over state, local and county law enforcement units, already. He also got that they were dragging their feet, spending their time profiling and evaluating evidence and following established protocols rather than getting eyes on the ground for a mile-by-mile search.

Sawyer silenced the drumming of his

fingers and checked his watch. It was going on noon. Commissioner Shauna Cartwright-Masterson had made the introductions at 11:00 a.m., and this guy was still talking.

"With the breathing equipment, our three boys made it farther downriver than the original search grid anticipated. Once beyond our perimeter, they could have headed out in any direction. A unit patrolling the river recovered this on the north bank early this morning. Forensics ID'd a partial print belonging to Henry Brennerman. So we will assume that at least one of our fugitives survived. Again, until we have dead bodies accounted for, we're going to treat this as a manhunt and not a recovery operation. Every county in Missouri, and in the eight states surrounding us, have been put on alert. But since two of the fugitives have ties to the K.C. area, we're focusing…"

Holt was already several steps behind the game, as far as Sawyer was concerned. Sawyer and Seth Cartwright, whose regular partner was on paternity leave, had already been on the phone and on the streets, tapping into sources with known ties to the escapees. Former addresses. Legit and not so legit employers. Sawyer had even taken a detour by

Melissa's house and the diner where she worked, confirming with his own eyes that she'd gotten safely from one place to the other that morning, and that officers were on duty in both locations. But even with adjusting to less-than-familiar investigative styles of a temporary partner, Sawyer would bet good money that he and Seth had already covered more names and places than the agent up front who was still talking plans and strategies.

"A man can't make this kind of equipment in a prison cell. What does that tell you?" Holt set down the evidence bag and surveyed the room, waiting for a response.

Smug bastard. Talking as though KCPD didn't know how to find a perp or solve a case.

Sitting beside him, Sawyer's brother Atticus pointed a finger into the air to answer. "They had outside help. I assume you've already interviewed any state prison, county jail and courthouse personnel with access to the escapees who might have accepted a bribe to assist them?"

To those who didn't know him, Atticus Kincaid came across as a reserved, level-headed investigator who never let his emotions cloud his thinking or his moods. But Atticus knew a thing or two about betrayal—about a cop selling out a partner for a better deal, about a lover using a man as a stepping stone in her career. Atticus would have a clearer understanding than most about such a traitor—and Sawyer recognized the undertones of smarter-than-you sarcasm in his brother's cool voice.

Sawyer had to prop his elbows on the long table in front of them and fold his hands over his mouth to hide his smirk from Special Agent Holt. "Nice one," he muttered.

Atticus pulled out his reading glasses and polished them with his handkerchief to hide his own retort. "Just helping him pause long enough to breathe the same air as the rest of us."

Holt nodded. Gibe or not, it was a legitimate question. And the man did love the sound of his own voice. "We're working our way through a list now. Thus far, the only suspicious sum we've run across is in a retirement fund belonging to one of the slain guards. We have a forensic accountant trying to pick up a money trail, but in the meantime, we're working other angles."

"And you've explored any connection the three fugitives themselves might share?

Other than Longbow and Brennerman being cell mates this past week, is there any commonality?" Sawyer silently cheered the follow-up question. Atticus was nothing if not thorough.

Holt's gaze narrowed on the dark-haired duo sitting in the front row, perhaps finally hearing the edge in Atticus's voice. "We're working on it."

Yeah, Holt and his crew seemed to be *working* on a lot of things.

But just as quickly as the challenge was noted, Holt dismissed it and turned his attention to the young woman sitting at a small table in the back corner of the room, who'd been busily taking notes throughout the briefing. "Miss Hansford? The handouts, please?"

Like a plain brown wren startled from its hiding place, Brooke Hansford glanced up from her laptop, looking surprised to see the room's attention thrown her way. Her fingers froze for an instant over the keyboard before adjusting her wire-framed glasses on the bridge of her nose. "Yes, sir."

Tucking a stray tendril into the tumble of mousy-brown hair pinned at the back of her head, the extraordinarily efficient Brooke— who, for two years, had kept John Kincaid's office organized and running as smoothly as a top-notch computer program—picked up a stack of folders and walked up and down the aisles, distributing them.

"These are the profiles that we've been able to put together thus far on our fugitives." Riley Holt continued, demanding the room's attention up front again. "All three committed different crimes. They come from different backgrounds, different ethnicity. Right now my team is interviewing…"

Sawyer shoved his fingers through his hair and sat up straight against the back of his chair. Just as quickly as he'd settled, he leaned toward Atticus and whispered, "His team, our team. Taking over Dad's secretary as his own—he's treating us like a bunch of lackeys."

"As long as we get these bastards, Sawyer. Any one of them could do some real damage. And if they're working together…"

"Here you go." Brooke had reached the front row and held out a black folder.

Sawyer winked as he took the file from her. "Thanks, Brooke."

"Sure thing." Her shy smile broadened to acknowledge Atticus, as well. "One for you, too."

His brother took the papers with a nod

and kept right on talking. "What really scares me is if all three of them are working *for* somebody."

Perhaps sensing the focus of the room was shifting, Agent Holt invited himself into the conversation. "That occurred to me as well, Detective, uh…" He paused to read the name on Atticus's ID tag. "Kincaid. I appreciate your comments. Perhaps you could offer us some insight into how these criminal minds work."

Though he knew damn well that Atticus could take care of himself, Sawyer scooted forward at the unspoken taunt. "How much longer is this going to take? Those three are going further underground with each passing minute."

"Down, big guy." Atticus held up his hand to warn Sawyer off. In the same unhurried motion he turned back to Agent Holt. "I do have some thoughts."

"I'd be interested in hearing them. Make an appointment with my assistant." Holt touched Brooke's shoulder. "Will you dim the lights for us, Miss Hansford?"

Brooke's cheeks colored as she ducked away from the touch or the claim or both, and hurried over to the light switch by the door.

As the lights dimmed, the room hushed and Holt pulled up a computer image on the screen behind him.

Sawyer relied on osmosis to take in the last of Holt's presentation. Once he turned to the most recent photos of Longbow, his thoughts drifted away into the past, when Ace was working as a dubious pit boss at the casino where Sawyer had tended bar.

Six foot six. Nearly three hundred pounds. A rap sheet of petty and violent crimes, ranging from unpaid parking tickets to multiple counts of assault and witness intimidation. A murder charge had been pled down to voluntary manslaughter, no doubt part of the deal he'd made in exchange for turning on Wolfe.

How did a brute like that wind up with a petite package of femininity like Melissa Teague? And how could that monster have ever produced a pint-size pistol like Benjamin?

Imagining Longbow standing next to Melissa and dwarfing her tiny frame—much less laying those big, meaty paws on her— took Sawyer to a very dark place inside him. A place not so far away from the bile that churned inside at the thought of his father's senseless murder. His nostrils flared as his breath quickened and his own hand curled into a fist.

Thank you for informing me. We'll be fine.

It wasn't right that Melissa had to stand up and be tough while Longbow ran free. Settling for a backup role in protecting her didn't feel right. He should be standing between her and the fear and danger her ex brought into her life. That's what his gun and badge and big, badass self were for.

Sawyer felt a light punch at his shoulder. "Earth to Detective Dreamy. We're done." The projector up front had been turned off, the lights turned on, and the sounds of sliding chairs and purposeful footsteps grew louder as Sawyer became aware of his surroundings again. Atticus's steel-gray eyes peered over the top of his glasses at him. "You okay?"

"No." Buying a moment to get his game face back into place, Sawyer closed the folder on Longbow's cold-eyed image, and did his damnedest to close off the memory of Melissa's stoic dismissal as well. "Did you just call me *Dreamy*, Brainiac Boy?"

Atticus smirked at the comeback before standing and tucking his glasses into the inside pocket of his blazer. "I know these three are trouble that nobody in Kansas City needs. But I can't help but note that the more manpower KCPD devotes to their capture, the fewer people there are looking for Dad's killer. The trail's only going to get colder the longer it takes to find a lead."

"I won't give up. Neither will Holden." Sawyer grabbed his leather jacket off the back of his chair and shrugged into it. He couldn't speak for Edward's commitment to uncovering the truth these days, but Sawyer was determined enough for all four of them. "You been stewing over things, too?"

Atticus nodded and followed him toward the exit. "Every waking moment. Even a few when I'm not awake."

"We'll get him," Sawyer vowed.

"Amen."

By the time the crowd had dispersed enough for them to reach the door, Sawyer felt a soft tug on the sleeve of his jacket. He turned to look down into the owlish expression on Brooke Hansford's face. "Do you have a second?" she asked.

"Sure." With a gentle nudge, he scooted her out of the path of the remaining officers lining up to leave the room. "What's up?"

She hugged the extra folders she carried

against her chest. "Would you tell your mom that I've gathered some personal items from John's office? I can take the box by the house this evening if she doesn't mind having a visitor. Otherwise, I can just run and get it for you now."

"Mom would probably enjoy the company. I'll give her a call and let her know you'll be stopping by."

"Thanks."

"Hey—Brainiac." He grabbed Atticus and pulled him aside to join them. Atticus might be the brother with the master's degree in criminology, but Sawyer had always been able to think on his feet. And an idea had just popped into his head. As loyal as Brooke had been to their father, she might be the key to getting them around departmental red tape. "Do you still have access to Dad's files?"

"He closed out all his cases or transferred them because of his promotion... Oh." Brooke's eyes widened as she realized what Sawyer was asking of her. "You want me to see if I can find anything suspicious?"

Catching on quickly, Atticus bent his head forward and whispered, "It should be easy enough. I heard Riley Holt moved all of Dad's stuff into your office so that he can use Dad's desk. Hell, his chair's not even cold yet."

Brooke nodded, clearing her throat when Atticus moved closer. "Agent Holt says he likes having a door he can lock. With room to spread out so his men and all their maps and charts and computers can fit in."

Sweeping in and taking over the space their father had earned? One more reason to resent the hotshot agent. With the prim-and-proper secretary standing there, though, he huffed out a deep breath instead of a curse. "Do you mind poking through things to see if anything jumps out at you? Homicide won't let us anywhere near Dad's paper-work."

Brooke might be a relatively young woman, but she'd been with the department long enough to understand why John Kincaid's sons weren't allowed to be an active part of the investigation. She'd also been a friend of the family long enough to understand how important this was to them. "It'll take me some time to get through all his papers and computer files—well, the ones that homicide hasn't confiscated yet. But I promise to work on them whenever Agent Holt doesn't need me."

"That'd be great. I know Mom appreciates you taking care of Dad's things here. We sure do."

"I loved John, too, you know. Sometimes I think he hired me as his assistant because he thought I needed a father figure in my life. Maybe even more than *he* needed my computer skills." She wiggled her nose against a telltale sniffle. "I think maybe I did. He was good to me."

Atticus reached out and rubbed his hand up and down her arm. "If you hear anything from homicide about their investigation, will you keep us posted?"

Her chin darted upward. "Sure." A soft smile crept across her mouth, brightening her plain features. "They don't keep me directly in the loop, but if I hear something—"

"Miss Hansford?" Riley Holt leaned in through the briefing room's doorway and gestured for her to follow him. "We need to get started."

"I'll be right there." She offered up an apologetic smile. "I have to go."

Brooke was already scurrying around him, so he called out some teasing advice. "Don't let him work you too hard, kiddo. And thanks."

With a nod, she disappeared through the

doorway. Sawyer shoved his hands into the pockets of his jacket. "Is it just me, or is there something not to like about Superagent Holt?"

"I just hope he's as good at his job as he thinks he is." Atticus straightened his tie and led the way down the hall toward the bank of elevators. "You up for some lunch? I figured we could go by the house and eat leftovers from last night's potluck with Mom. Check on her and give Holden a break. Maybe pack up some food to take by Edward's, too. I imagine he's drinkin' his way through this. Hell. I was almost surprised to see him at the funeral yesterday."

"Nah. He'd do a lot of things, but he wouldn't hurt Mom by not showing up." The center elevator doors opened and a federal agent, dressed in a suit and tie similar to Riley Holt's stepped off. But when Sawyer moved aside to let him pass, he halted in his tracks. "What the hell...?"

BEHIND THE FIRST AGENT came a second one, with his hand firmly wrapped around Melissa Teague's upper arm. "I'm telling you, I don't know anything. I haven't seen him or talked to him in months."

"Mel?"

He blocked their path and her blue eyes tilted up and locked on to his.

"Sawyer."

He glared at the hand on her arm, then at the agent holding her. "Is that necessary?"

The suit released her and held out his hands as though he'd done Sawyer a favor. "I'm just escorting the lady in, as ordered."

"I'll take a rain check on lunch, Atticus."

His brother had already lined up beside him. "You got this covered?"

"It's covered."

Melissa's damp hair clung to her cheek. "Sawyer, please don't make a big deal out of this."

"What exactly *is* this?" He sought out her unblinking gaze again. "Are you all right?"

"I'm fine." She pushed her hair off her face with a frustrated sigh, then just as quickly, shook her head to hide that damn scar again. *Fine* didn't cover the tight fist that clutched together the front of her tan raincoat. "If I'm a little jumpy, it's because they came to pick me up in the middle of the lunch rush. I feel guilty about leaving Pearl, my boss, short-handed, that's all." Below the hem of her damp coat, he could see she wore the light blue dress and sensible tan shoes she worked in. "They want me to tell them about Ace."

"I'll catch up with you later." Atticus announced his departure, making sure the agents knew he was taking his time to circle behind them and push the button to call the elevator back. He wasn't in any hurry to leave if his brother needed backup.

"She doesn't know anything," Sawyer insisted.

"I think we'll let Mrs. Longbow tell us that."

Sawyer shook his head as the cool, friendly-on-the-surface voice of Riley Holt sounded in the hallway behind him.

"I'm Special Agent Riley Holt, ma'am." The FBI's golden-haired golden boy brushed past and placed his hand at the small of Melissa's back. "If you'll come this way."

The urge to grab the man and hold him back fisted through Sawyer's hands, but he kept them at his sides as Holt and his armed entourage took Melissa away. "It's Miss *Teague*," he emphasized, slowly turning to keep them in his sight. Holt paused, glancing back and arching an eyebrow at the interruption. *That's right, hotshot. The big dumb cop knows stuff, too.* "She hasn't gone by Mrs. Longbow since her divorce nearly two years ago."

"How did you…?" He zeroed in on Melissa's soft gasp and watched her surprise transform into a more guarded posture. "He's right. I use my maiden name so my son and I share the same legal last name. I have full custody."

"Of Longbow's son?" Holt prodded.

"*My* son." *Brava, Melissa.* With her chin tipped up and that sharp tone of voice, she seemed half a foot taller.

"Longbow's name is on the birth certificate."

"Ace has never been a father to him."

"My mistake." With a deferring nod, Holt gestured down the hallway. "If you'll come this way and answer a few questions, you can clear up any other misconceptions we might have. Good day, Detective."

"What do you mean by 'misconceptions'?" Melissa asked.

But Holt was already guiding her forward, into the office that still read John Kincaid, Deputy Chief.

Sawyer wasn't about to be dismissed. He followed the two escort agents into the office and closed the door himself.

"What the hell are you doing?" Holt's golden boy veneer was slipping.

Sawyer crossed his arms over his chest

and shrugged as though he was doing them a favor by standing guard. "Helping out. You *did* say this manhunt was going to be a joint departmental effort."

"And here I didn't think you were listening during my briefing. Miss Teague." Agent Holt pulled out a chair for Melissa and directed the other two to flank him. Sawyer breathed evenly and deeply. The intimidation tactic wasn't going to work. And the sympathetic words that came next just pissed him off. "I understand you and your brother have recently suffered a tragic loss. I'm sorry to hear about your father, Detective. But your…grief…seems to be affecting your attitude. I told you we were interviewing anyone with a connection to our fugitives. Perhaps it's better if you leave this sensitive task to someone with a cooler head."

"She's *ex*-wife. There's no connection."

"Not according to her attorney. Miss Teague still has an active restraining order against Longbow to prevent any mail or telephone contact. That tells me he'll make an effort to get in touch with her if he can."

"So you drag her down to headquarters like *she's* some kind of suspect? Sounds like Longbow's problem, not hers."

Melissa rose from her chair. "Sawyer, don't—"

"No one forced her to come. My men made it clear that she could answer our questions here or at work."

"You want to drag up the past in front of her friends and her boss? That's not much of a choice."

Nudging her way past Holt, Melissa reached out and tapped her fingers against the front of Sawyer's jacket. "I know you're trying to help me. But I have to be home in a couple of hours to stay with Benjamin so that Mom can get to her part-time job. I called my attorney from the diner and he's on his way. Please. I just want to get this over and done with as quickly as possible."

Holt frowned behind her. "We'll be as quick as we can be, ma'am. But you do realize we're talking about three cop killers here, don't you?"

"I know better than anyone the kind of damage Ace can do. I'm here, aren't I?"

"Do this another time, Holt," Sawyer warned.

"There is no other time with those three on the loose. Now, will you step out so we can get started? Or do I have to throw you out?"

Sawyer didn't budge. He looked from man to man to the woman standing between them. He didn't like the odds. "Three agents to interview one woman? I'm not moving unless Mel tells me to go."

The fingers resting so lightly against his chest curled into the leather of his jacket. Sawyer dropped his gaze at the subtle demand. One moment she was reaching out to him, letting him read the helpless resignation in her eyes that reminded him of how isolated, how unsettled she must feel to be caught up in the nightmare that was Ace Longbow all over again.

The next moment, that mask slid back into place and she released him.

"I want you to go."

Chapter Four

Melissa turned her head from the emotion that darkened Sawyer's eyes and set his mouth in a grim line. "I'm sorry. But I don't want you here."

She knew he was only trying to help. He wanted to support her, befriend her. Back at the casino when they'd worked together, he'd always been ready to jump in when Ace would come around and fire verbal warning shots, or when their boss's hands started to wander a little too familiarly over his female employees.

But her ex-husband had only wanted to take care of her, too. She wouldn't make the mistake of trusting a man to protect her again. And while the intuitive part of her brain tried to tell her that Sawyer wouldn't hurt her, the logical side reminded her that she'd never suspected Ace would harm her before that first time, either.

Besides, she couldn't surrender her independence. And if she started relying on someone now, when the FBI only wanted to ask her questions, how could she possibly find the strength to stand on her own two feet when faced with a more difficult, more dangerous challenge? She shouldn't be looking for a shoulder to lean on.

"You're sure?" Sawyer asked. His deep, husky tone reached down to her like an invisible caress, speeding her pulse and awakening something feminine deep inside her.

She shouldn't be looking for *that*, either.

Silently, she nodded.

"Well, Kincaid, it looks as though the decision to leave has been made for you. Allow me to get the door." Melissa jumped when Riley Holt's body brushed against hers as he reached around her for the doorknob. "I'll give you points for tenacity. But if we're going to find Longbow and the others, it'll require a little finesse." He pulled the door open a few inches, releasing it with a tight smile when the wooden frame hit Sawyer's foot and stopped. With a subtle twist, Melissa moved away from the faintly territorial feel of Agent Holt's lingering proximity. "I appreciate you and the rest of KCPD providing the manpower to give us eyes all around the city. Ultimately, though, those fugitives are my responsibility. So we'll do things my way."

"Nice speech, Holt."

Though her gaze had fixed on the black-ribboned badge hanging from a chain at the center of Sawyer's chest, she felt his eyes sweeping her face one last time. But before she gave in to the request to meet his probing gaze, he turned and walked out the door, closing it firmly behind him.

"I apologize for the unpleasantness, Miss Teague. Very unprofessional. If you'll have a seat, we can get started. I don't think there's anyone who can give us more insight into what Longbow might be thinking or planning than you. Shall we?" Agent Holt and his men quickly moved to triangulated positions around the office, leaving her standing at the center, not unlike a wolf pack circling its prey.

Melissa shivered as the discomfiting image popped into her imagination. Girding her mental and emotional armor, she knotted the belt of her trench coat more tightly around her waist. A secretarial-type woman with thick glasses and a sympathetic look sat beside Agent Holt's desk, her pen and notepad poised at the ready to record whatever useful information Melissa gave them.

She'd been questioned like this before, reporting Ace's second attack, once she learned the first one hadn't been a fluke. She'd been questioned again by attorneys when she'd filed for divorce. And again by KCPD and others when it turned out her second attempt at a relationship hadn't been much smarter than the first. Teddy Wolfe didn't hit her, but when Ace had threatened to harm their son if she didn't get him hired by the casino owner, she should have known there was something illegal going on. Teddy turned out to be involved in organized crime, and Ace made a perfect thug to carry out his orders. She'd answered questions about those activities, too.

"Miss Teague?"

She gripped the belt a little tighter. Sawyer's chest had been wide and solid beneath her fingertips, and the warmth she'd felt had beckoned her to move closer. Just a little. She felt so cold right now. So small. So alone.

And the wolves were circling.

"Sit. Please."

Sit, little one. I'm talkin' now. Sit!

Melissa jerked as if the remembered slap across the face had been real.

She grabbed the door and swung it open. "Wait." She dashed into the hall, spotted the dark head and broad shoulders at the elevator. "Sawyer, wait!"

"Miss Teague!"

Ignoring Riley Holt's shout of protest, she hurried toward the elevators. Frowning, Sawyer turned and met her halfway. "What's wrong?"

His warm grasp swallowed up both of her hands that reached for him. *I want you to hold me. I want you to back me up. I want…* She fought off the urge to keep moving forward. As welcome as she suspected she'd be, snugged up against the abundant strength of Sawyer's chest, she still had to stand on her own two feet. "Will you do me a favor?"

His expression changed, softened. "Name it."

Melissa swallowed hard. She knew he'd be disappointed by her request, that he had this whole macho thing about protecting *her*. But if he *really* wanted to help… And she really could use a friend right about now.

"Would you stop by the house and stay with Benjamin and Mom until she leaves for work this afternoon? If I'm running late, she'll have to take him to the store with her and—" Melissa pressed her lips together and breathed to stop the rambling. "They, um, like you. You were quite the topic at breakfast this morning. And, Mom's nervous enough about Ace—"

"And you're not?"

"I know she'd feel safer with a man around. Someone she knows. I'll try to get home as soon as I can, but—"

"Hey." The hand holding hers squeezed gently, cutting through the spew of panic and fear that had bubbled to the surface. "Don't worry about your family. I'll stay there."

The controlling fist that had been squeezing her lungs eased its grip on her. She inhaled a deep breath and held it, not sure if she should trust the relief she felt. "You don't mind?"

"As long as you're sure you'll be okay here, I don't mind babysitting. Or mom-sitting."

Melissa searched his expression for signs of sarcasm, but saw nothing but a matter-of-fact sincerity there. It couldn't be that simple, could it? There had to be a catch to his easy cooperation. "This doesn't mean anything—between you and me," she clarified. "But I would appreciate the help."

Agent Holt muttered impatiently from the doorway behind her. "The clock is ticking, Miss Teague…"

Sawyer glanced over the top of her head, no doubt sending a silent message to her interrogator about what he could do with his clock, before dropping his gaze back to hers. "Don't sweat it, Mel. This is just one friend doing a favor for another." He hunched down, bringing his conspiratorial grin down to her level to whisper, "Though, say the word, and I'd be happy to take out Holt's pompous ass if you want me to."

An unexpected giggle bubbled up in her throat and she pressed her knuckles to her mouth to stifle it. That's when Melissa realized that she was still clinging to Sawyer's hand.

Melissa didn't make a habit of laughing. She didn't make a habit of holding on to a man as though he was some kind of lifeline, either.

Gathering her composure, sliding her survival armor back into place, Melissa released her grip and stuffed her traitorous hands into her pockets. "He's just doing his job." The elevator doors opened behind Sawyer and she recognized the balding, middle-aged man who stepped out. "My attorney, Mr. Landon, is here. I'll be all right. Thank you."

"Don't worry about anything on the home front. And don't let Holt railroad you into saying or doing anything you're not comfortable with." Sawyer gave the agent one of those man-to-man looks that spoke of challenges and ownership and respecting boundaries that had always spelled disaster with her ex. Then Sawyer turned to her attorney and pointed a finger. "You. Stay with her until they're done."

Frank Landon's eyes widened, startled by the directness of the order. "Of course."

And then Sawyer reached out—to touch her hair, or possibly her face. But Melissa's self-conscious flinch was enough to make any man—correction, any man but Ace—draw his hand away. Sawyer nodded, reluctantly curling his fingers into his palm and accepting the odd sort of truce she'd offered by asking him to help her at all. "I'll see you later."

Clearly he wasn't comfortable with leaving her to face the wolves with only her attorney to protect her, but truth be told, she'd faced worse all by her lonesome. At least this time, she wouldn't have to worry about her mother freaking out when she heard that her daughter was down at the police station. Again. Sawyer did seem to have a way with Fritzi Teague—calming her, making her laugh and forget the stresses of her life for a moment.

As she watched him return to the elevator, Melissa realized he'd had a similar effect on her.

She nodded to her attorney, then turned to face Riley Holt. She pulled her shoulders back and walked into the room. Holding herself ramrod straight, she sat down. "I'm ready."

Let the inquisition begin.

"HOLD TIGHT, Big Ben." Sawyer lifted his assistant carpenter in the crook of one arm, and guided the small battery-powered drill to the second screw that would anchor the new window lock into place. "Now I'll hold it and you squeeze the trigger like I showed you."

Benjamin Teague squinched up his expression beneath the plastic safety goggles that covered half his face. This boy was very serious about his power tools.

"Vroom-vroom!" He mimicked the sound of the drill as he spun the screw three-fourths of the way into the wood with nary a slip or scratch.

"Just a little more," Sawyer coached. "Squeeze."

"Vroom—oh!"

He kept a firm hold on both boy and drill when the screw head hit the metal base and stopped. Startled by the sudden jolt, Benjamin let go. But his surprise was quickly replaced by delighted laughter at his success.

"Good job, buddy." Sawyer set the boy down and traded high fives, laughing right along with him.

With Melissa's house feeling about as secure as he could make it with the tools and supplies he had on hand, and his stomach full of the meat loaf and real mashed potatoes Fritzi had started before she left that afternoon, Sawyer was in a pretty good mood himself.

He suspected the invitation to join them for a late dinner was Melissa's way of thanking him for staying with Benjamin for an hour after her mother had left for work. He didn't think it was because his company made her feel secure and relaxed, not if the stiff posture and stilted conversation over the hearty, home-cooked meal was any indication. She'd probably shooed him from the kitchen and insisted on washing the dishes herself afterward, too, not because she was the hostess and he was the guest, but because she needed a break from having to pretend that she was comfortable having him take up so much space in her tiny kitchen.

Though she'd held on to his hand at the police station like she wanted him to be her hero, her words had made it clear that he wasn't supposed to read anything personal into asking him for a favor. Melissa claimed she didn't want his help for herself, but she seemed to be a little less uptight about having a man around the house if he was there for her mother and son. And Sawyer was certainly enjoying his time with Benjamin. Doing the small repair projects together reminded him of good times spent with his father, learning simple skills like how to bait a fishhook, throw a baseball or replace bent and rusting hardware around the house.

For a short while, he wasn't even thinking of his father's murder or how much he missed him. He was living in the moment. His favor for Melissa was turning out to be a gift to himself—a respite from turbulent thoughts and ugly emotions and his frustrated sense of justice.

Plus, he certainly appreciated the bonus of seeing Mel dressed in something besides work clothes. Worn jeans and a plain V-neck sweater weren't as provocative as the low-cut cocktail waitress getup she'd once worked in. But seeing the soft cotton gently hug and move with every delectable curve of her figure had had his body on a slow simmer since his first helping of potatoes.

When she'd gotten home from KCPD headquarters, she'd hugged Benjamin first and talked with him about his day. Then she'd disappeared for a few minutes to wash her face and change into her casual clothes. She'd pulled her hair back into a ponytail, and though there were a few loose strands that cupped her cheek, she hadn't once touched her scar or tried to hide it from him. To Sawyer's way of thinking, her beauty hadn't changed all that much from the first time he'd met her. If anything, it had matured like a fine wine, going to his head more quickly and making him want more than just a taste.

But he'd do his damnedest not to push. He'd content himself with the notion that twenty-four hours ago, she couldn't get him out of her house fast enough. But tonight, she'd not only asked him to help her while she was gone, but she had allowed him to stay and get a glimpse of the real woman she'd always kept so well hidden in the past.

"Are you two working men done out here?" Sweet reality walked into the living room, drying her hands on a dish towel. And even though her eyes were focused on her son, Melissa's smile was serene and gorgeous and made Sawyer feel like smiling himself. Her lips rounded into a surprised "Oh" when she saw the big bug eyes of the goggles on Ben's face. "My goodness, it's a little man from outer space."

"It's me, Mommy."

"Of course it's you, silly. I'd know my Benjamin anywhere."

"I used the hammer and the plastic things…" Sawyer straightened beside his sidekick as Benjamin grabbed a handful of wall anchors and stuck them on the ends of his fingers. The boy launched into a report of the exciting new skills he'd learned. "And the best was the dwill. And I scwewed the scwews. *Vroom!*"

"Power tools are a man's best friend,"

Sawyer sagely joked at the little boy's enthusiasm.

"'Scwewed the scwews'?" Melissa mimicked.

Sawyer caught a glimpse of a smile before she turned away—just like that laugh she'd made such an effort to hide down at KCPD headquarters that afternoon. He wondered if Melissa had laughed a lot before the day she'd met Longbow. The impulse was there. But she kept such tight control over what part of herself she revealed to people. That scar was out there on her face for all the world see and judge. Maybe keeping her thoughts and emotions and sense of humor hidden away was as much a form of protection as the unlisted phone number and reluctance to get involved with another man might be.

Don't push.

"Thank you for all your hard work, Benjamin."

"'Tawyer, too."

"And Sawyer, too." Melissa plucked a trio of plastic anchors from Benjamin's fingers and tossed them into Sawyer's toolbox as she folded her little boy's hand into her own. "But it's time for bed. Say good night, sweetie."

"Good night, sweetie," Sawyer dutifully responded.

"'Night, tweetie," Ben repeated. The four-year-old was too young to get the joke, but the smile was there, teasing the corner of Melissa's mouth again.

Sawyer watched her shoulders expand with a deep, controlling breath. When she glanced back up, the smile was gone. "Do you mind hanging around for a few minutes longer while I put him to bed?"

"You want me to make sure your mom gets home okay?"

"Something like that. She works until eight. Do you mind? Or, if you have some-place you need to be, I understand."

Something like that? Sawyer wasn't smiling anymore, either. The reprieve was over. Suspicions and concerns and the need to be on guard instantly returned.

"Staying's no problem. I'll clean up here and take the toolbox back to my truck. I'll lock the door behind me, so you'll have to let me in." He reached down and tapped Ben's nose and then the goggles. "Would you like to keep those?"

"Oh no, we can't accept—"

"My gift," he insisted, silencing Melissa's

protest. He combed his fingers through the delicate silk of Ben's black hair and ruffled it out of place. "In exchange for letting me hang out and think about normal things for a while."

Melissa's questioning frown at his cryptic comment was just as subtle as her smile had been. And it disappeared just as quickly. She nudged Benjamin forward. "What do you say to Detective Kincaid?"

"Tanks, 'Tective!"

"You're welcome."

"Can I sleep in my goggas, Mommy?"

"We'll see."

Benjamin "vroomed" all the way down the hall to the bedrooms at the back of the house.

Sawyer watched mother and son every step of the way, wondering if these pangs of wanting to stay in this tiny house and never leave were anything like what his father had felt when he was involved in a case that demanded so much of his time and focus. He used to suspect that having an equally busy wife and four boys running around the house only compounded the stress.

But tonight Sawyer wondered if that sometimes peaceful, sometimes crazy escape into family dinners and home repairs, baseball games and camping trips—no matter how brief it had been—was what had sustained John Kincaid throughout his long and abruptly terminated career.

It was one of many questions he'd never be able to ask his father now.

Venting gut-deep regret on one low, painful sigh, Sawyer packed his toolbox, then retrieved his gun and holster from the mantel where he'd set them beyond Benjamin's reach. The storms were giving it a rest for a couple of hours, but the night sky was black and moonless, heavy with clouds waiting to drop more moisture onto the rain-soaked city. Blending into the night himself with his dark jeans and leather jacket, Sawyer held up his shiny brass and nickel badge, identifying himself to the officer sitting in the squad car across the street.

With a squint and a salute, the officer went back to the paper he was reading and Sawyer loaded his toolbox in the back of his truck. *Damn rookie.* Though Sawyer knew from firsthand experience how tedious a stakeout could be, the kid should be focused on taking note of any activity along the street, not catching up on the sports page.

After a quick survey up and down the

block himself, Sawyer jogged over to the squad car and rapped on the roof. The interior light came on as the young officer folded his paper and rolled down the window. "Cho, is it? I'm Sawyer Kincaid, Fourth Precinct."

"Yes, sir. Is there something I can do for you?"

He just wanted to keep the kid on his toes. "How long have you been here?"

"I came on a couple hours ago. My shift ends at eight in the morning."

"Been pretty quiet?" Sawyer wasn't making small talk to pass the time. He spotted the printout of Ace Longbow's mug shot on the passenger seat, and sized up just how young and inexperienced Officer Cho seemed to be.

"Yes, sir. Looks like the neighbors have pretty much turned in for the night. The only cars going by have been through traffic. No rentals. No license plates that pop up as stolen. And nobody's slowed down to take a look at the house."

Not such a rookie, after all. "Good. Stay sharp, Cho." He nodded toward the flyer on the far seat. "I don't think our man Longbow is big on stealth. But if he gets past you, he'll be next to impossible to bring down."

"Understood."

Sawyer reached into the leather wallet behind his badge and pulled out a business card. "Do me a favor. I've got a personal interest in Miss Teague. If you do see anything suspicious, give me a call at any of these numbers."

The young man took the card and tucked it into the pocket of his blue uniform shirt. "Will do, sir."

With a nod of thanks, Sawyer put the officer back to work. With the feds nosing around and Sawyer signed on as unofficial backup, they should be able to stay one step ahead of Longbow.

He just prayed that *should* would be enough to keep Melissa and her family safe.

"IN HERE, BRENNERMAN!"

Ace Longbow leaned his good shoulder into the locked office door and shoved it open, while Hank packed up the laptop and cords that had helped them bypass the security system at the entrance to the Armour Boulevard Sports Emporium.

The shorter man slipped past him and pulled up a chair to the desk inside the biggest cubicle. "You're bleedin' again, Ace."

"Just get on the damn computer and look up what I told you." While Hank turned on the computer and did his thing, Ace went back out to the store floor and pulled a towel off a golf-club display. The pain in his shoulder had ebbed to a dull ache, but apparently tonight's activities had ripped out the clumsy stitches Tyrell had put in him. He glanced down at the spots of blood seeping through the gauze bandage and plaid shirt, grit his teeth and pressed the towel against his wound.

The woman who'd given birth to him had come after him with a broken beer bottle one time when he'd accidentally burst in on her and one of her friends having a "party," as she'd called them. He'd been eight years old, and in a lot of ways, that cut had hurt a hell of a lot worse than the bullet in his shoulder. Blood or not, this wound wasn't going to stop him.

He made his way back to the doorway and rested against the frame so that he could keep an eye on both the front door and Hank. "Found the personnel files yet?"

"I'm lookin'," Hank answered. "This is takin' longer than the job I did for Tyrell's friend. Breakin' into three different stores, lookin' for some old woman. I shouldn't be here. Tyrell's friend made it very clear that we weren't supposed to be together. I could be on my way out of the country by now if you hadn't tracked me down." He looked up with that ugly gap-toothed grin. "Must be the Indian half of ya."

Must be because he'd made a career out of tracking down people and convincing them to do whatever he or his employer wanted them to do. Maybe this new boss could put those same talents to use in his organization.

Ace let the half-breed comment slide. "You had seventy-two hours to make payback. Nobody said you had to finish the job on the first day."

"I don't like to waste time, no sir. I'm ready to be in Mexico with a bottle of tequila. Besides, I could have broken into KCPD's computer system and altered the lab reports on those names with one hand tied behind my back. They'd never even know I was there. Trust me, I've got nothin' but helpin' you keepin' me here in K.C."

"You talk too much."

"Helps me think. Clears the clutter out of my brain."

If it would move him along any faster... "I thought you had a girlfriend in town."

"Trust me, the babes in Mexico'll be prettier." Hank laughed. "Why don't you just do what you're supposed to, then come with me. They have doctors down there who can take care of you. Some mighty fine nurses, too, I'll bet."

"It's Fritzi T-E-A-G-U-E. See if the biddy-in-law is in the system."

Hank looked at the screen again. "Tyrell's friend is gonna be pissed that we've been breakin' into places tonight. I wonder what they're doin' to keep the cops from finding us. I've seen our faces all over the news."

"You disabled the security cameras here, didn't you?"

"Yeah."

"Then I don't care about Tyrell or his friend."

Seemed Hank was doing a lot more talking than typing. "I overheard Tyrell talkin' to his friend about some cop's murder. You know anything about that?"

"I'm not interested in any cop. Have you found the employee information yet?"

"He said you knew him—that's why he gave Tyrell the job to clean up some loose ends on that hit instead of you."

"Seth Cartwright's the cop who put me in jail. He's the one I'd want to see dead."

"Cartwright…Cartwright… That sounds familiar."

Ace swore. "Have you found her name yet?"

"Here's an employee application file." Ace straightened while Hank clicked and scrolled through the information. "I don't know why we're hittin' sporting goods stores to find your mother-in-law's name. Seems like a funny place for an old lady to work."

"She's not that old. Fifty-five, sixty, maybe. She runs marathons. If she's still workin', it'd be in a place like this." Tracking down Fritzi would be easier than checking all the restaurants and bars throughout the city to find where Melissa was working now. "Well?"

Hank snapped his fingers. "Cartwright's *boss*. That's where I heard the name. Tyrell's friend put a hit on Cartwright's boss— Deputy Commissioner Kincaid. His was one of the reports I changed, too. I guess Kincaid and Tyrell's friend used to work together, or something like that—doesn't want any connection made between them."

"Great. You got your gossip straight. Have you found a name?"

"Yes!" Hank pumped his fists in victory as he read the screen. "It says, 'F' Teague. Is that her?"

Ace grabbed a notepad and pen off the closest desk. "What's the address?"

He copied down the name of the street. With his name and face plastered all over the news, the cops would probably be watching the house. But if he could find the address, he could find a way to get past security, too.

"You want the phone number, Ace?"

"It's probably her attorney's number—816-555—"

"Nope. This one has a 461 prefix."

"Give it to me."

After reading off the number, Hank asked, "Is it okay if I shut down now?"

Ace rubbed his thumb across the numbers on the notepad, feeling something calm and gentle wash over him. He was that much closer to the woman he loved. "Yeah."

Melissa's phone number. He'd figure out a way to get around any cops at her house tomorrow. But he could talk to her tonight.

But not here. Someplace private.

Ace pocketed the entire notepad so no one could trace the information he'd wanted. He stuffed the bloody towel into his pocket, too. He'd worn plastic gloves so he wouldn't leave any fingerprints behind—he wasn't about to make a dumb mistake by giving the cops any other way to find him.

In fact, there was only one thing he did intend to leave behind.

Hank turned off the computer and picked up his equipment bag. "So, I messed up KCPD's lab records, Tyrell's doing God knows what—what's your payback assignment?"

Ace pulled out his gun and shot Hank between the eyes. Then he stood over the body and put another slug in his heart.

"To get rid of you and Tyrell."

Chapter Five

A pot of decaf coffee and an hour spent re-capping Fritzi Teague's collection of customers around the kitchen table later, Sawyer was beginning to think Melissa didn't mind his company as much as she claimed.

True, Melissa had probably already heard the stories about how today's teenage athletes were so much more technologically and equipment savvy than in Fritzi's days back in high school when she had to compete on a private club because her school didn't even have organized girls' sports teams. But when staying to make sure Fritzi got home safely became "Mom tends to bake a lot when she's under stress, so there's a cherry pie if you're hungry again," Sawyer had to think there was more to Melissa's invitation than giving her mother a fresh ear for her stories.

But now the hour was late, the rain had resumed its steady cadence on the roof and Fritzi Teague was yawning again. "Oh, my." The older woman adjusted her glasses to check the time on her watch. "Heavens, it's nearly midnight." Sawyer stood as she pushed her chair back from the table and carried her empty plate and cup to the sink. "No wonder I can't stay awake."

Melissa followed with her coffee cup. "Leave them in the sink, Mom. I'll clean up."

"Oh no you won't." Fritzi took her daughter's cup and reached for Sawyer's, too. "I'll take care of them in the morning. You need to get to bed—you have to be at the diner at six a.m."

Sawyer wished he could see that soft, indulgent smile directed at him. "Fine. You win. You get to do the dishes. But, if you don't mind, I need to discuss something with Sawyer before I turn in."

"Oh?" Fritzi tilted her wink-wink grin up at him before turning back to Melissa. "Then I'll just head off to bed." The two women shared a hug. "Don't stay up too late, dear. If you need anything, you'll have to shake me to wake me up because I'll have my earplugs in. I won't be able to hear a thing."

The wattage of Fritzi's smile dimmed before saying good night. She had the heart to play matchmaker, but the presence of mind to remember that Sawyer wasn't exactly here on a social visit. "Is Officer Cho still watching the house?"

Sawyer nodded. "He'll be right out front all night long."

"Good. I'll rest a little easier. You don't think he'd want any pie, do you?"

"Maybe in the morning."

"I'll ask him then." She reached up and patted his shoulder. "You drop by and see us anytime."

He might not push his luck quite that much, but he appreciated the welcome from at least one woman in the house. On impulse, Sawyer bent and kissed her cheek. "Good night, Fritzi."

Fritzi cupped her cheek and laughed as she hurried out of the kitchen.

He waited until he heard her bedroom door close before turning his attention back to whatever Melissa was busying herself with now. "Earplugs? Do you snore?"

She'd crossed the kitchen to open the pantry door. "*She* does. Wakes herself up sometimes. I don't think all this rain is helping her allergies. Benjamin talks in his sleep sometimes, too. The doctor says it's a normal phase for a boy his age."

If Melissa hadn't mentioned wanting to discuss something with him, he'd have grabbed his jacket from the back of his chair and taken the cue to leave. But now she was moving cans and boxes aside to pull something from the back of the closet.

Was she worried about her son? "He's not having nightmares, is he?"

"I don't think so." She paused in her rear ranging. "Sometimes I sit in his room through the night and try to listen. Usually, it's gibberish. Maybe a word or two about a toy or game—I'm sure I'll hear *'Vroom-vroom'* tonight."

"Yeah."

She stepped farther into the closet. "I worry that he has memories of his father…and me." Sawyer bit down on his tongue. He didn't need to hear the details of her abusive marriage, but he could fill in the blanks. "He was so young when we were still married—just a baby, really. But he might have heard things."

"He heard, I'm sure. All my training says that when there's abuse, everyone in the home is affected."

"My counselor says that, too."

"Hopefully, he was too young to know what any of it meant."

Melissa went back to work. "He's never asked about his father, and I haven't brought up the subject. That's probably not fair, but I wouldn't know what to say. Ace never really interacted with him. I thought every man wanted a son. But he seemed to think Ben was a competitor for my attention. I was always so worried Ace would hurt him, out of jealousy—that's what finally gave me the courage to file for divorce. The situation wasn't safe for Benjamin."

"For you, either." Sawyer didn't trust himself to say much more until he got his opinion of Ace's fathering instincts under control.

"Here."

When Melissa turned around, he could see she held a small metal strongbox. "What's that?"

"Special Agent Holt seemed to think that Ace would try to contact me if he was alive. And to be honest, I figured he would, too. Since he hasn't, maybe he *did* drown in the river."

Sawyer leaned his hips back against the edge of her white tile counter, bringing him a few inches closer to her level. "Do you really believe that?"

"I have an unlisted phone number and a new job and address that he doesn't know about. I suspect it's just taking him longer to track me down than he'd counted on." Her tone took on that bleak resignation again. "But if he's alive…he's coming."

"I thought as much. Back at the casino, even though you guys were divorced, he seemed pretty possessive, pretty…focused… on you."

"That's my Ace. Whether he's feeling romantic or he needs someone to blame for his trouble, I seem to be his entire world."

Sawyer scrubbed at the stubble peppering his jaw and bit his tongue. What could he say about Ace Longbow's sick obsession that wouldn't come off sounding angry or possessive himself?

Melissa broke the awkward silence first. She set the box on the table and pulled a key from a drawer to open it. "When I was being questioned this afternoon, Agent Holt kept coming back to the letters Ace sent me from Jefferson City. He wanted them to see if they gave any indication of what Ace's plans might be. My attorney had most of them. He already turned them over to Agent Holt." Melissa opened the box and pulled out a stack of fifteen, maybe twenty, envelopes, held together by a thick rubber band. "These are the first ones he sent me. Before we moved out of my old apartment."

"How many letters are we talking about?"

"Nearly two hundred. Ace wrote to me almost every day he was incarcerated."

"That…" Sawyer's curse was both colorful and to the point. Melissa spun around, her cheeks pale, her eyes wide. "Thank God your mom couldn't hear that."

Melissa didn't laugh.

Though he regretted startling her, he damn sure wasn't going to apologize for his reaction to discovering another twisted dimension to Longbow's obsession with her. He paced off the width of the kitchen. Twice.

"I am not your ex-husband, Mel," he tried to explain. "People lose their tempers—and mine's been on an unusually short leash lately. It burns me to think about how depraved that bastard is. But that doesn't mean I'm going to make anybody else pay for me feeling this way." He wound up on the opposite side of the room again, giving her as much space as he could. "Quit looking at me as though I could hurt you in the same way he did. I get mad. But I don't abuse women. You're just gonna have to take that on faith, sweetheart. If you've got any faith left in you."

"It's not that."

"Normal people feel things. You're allowed to lose your temper, too, Mel. You're allowed to feel disgust, fear, anger, loss. You're allowed to feel good things, too. Laugh. Love. Get goofy sometimes."

"Goofy?"

"A real man isn't going to hurt you when he gets mad at the world, or something doesn't go his way. But you can't condemn him for feeling the emotions."

"I'm not condemning you. I know you're not Ace. But it's hard to trust when that level of emotion spins out of control and nearly gets you killed."

Sawyer held himself as still as he could, evening out his breathing and willing his pulse to slow back down. And when he looked—really looked—he saw it was regret, maybe even sadness, staring back at him from Melissa's eyes. But then she blinked and the emotions vanished altogether. The mask was back in place.

But it wasn't locked on tight.

Melissa watched her hands as she locked the box and put it away in the pantry. Sawyer watched them, too. They were a little bit shaky as they worked. And when that task was done, they continued to move—straightening her sweater, adjusting her ponytail, arranging the chairs just so as she circled the table.

The detachment in her voice was a little shaky, too. "When we moved here—I wanted Ben to have a yard he could play in—but I also wanted to disappear from Ace's life. Instead of forwarding our mail, I filed an order to have all of Ace's correspondence go to Mr. Landon's office." She pushed the stack of letters across the table to the side where Sawyer stood. "Would you give these to Agent Holt? I think he believes I'd help Ace."

"You wouldn't help that bastard," Sawyer insisted.

"No." She grasped the back of the chair in front of her as Sawyer came to retrieve them. "Obviously, there's nothing in them about an escape plan—they were written too long ago. But he does talk about threats he got in prison, about the contract Mr. Wolfe put out on him. Other stuff. I think Ace broke out because he saw that as the only way to save his own life. There might be something in there that could help Agent Holt with his manhunt. I don't want him to think I'm with-holding evidence."

"Did he say that?"

"Not in so many words. But three hours of interrogation? You tell me the FBI doesn't think I'm involved somehow. I don't think Riley Holt is interested in protecting me or my family. He wants to use me to find Ace."

"I'll protect you."

At last she tipped her chin up and looked him straight in the eye. "No one asked you to make a promise like that."

Had Ace damaged her so much, inside and out, that she couldn't believe any man's promise?

"I'll do it, anyway."

"I'm learning how to take care of myself and my family. I'm working to get a profes-sional job. Keeping a roof over our heads. I even took a self-defense course at the junior college. Not that a flyweight like me would have much of a chance against Ace. But I'm trying to be independent. I need my son to know that I can stand on my own two feet. That I don't have to be taken care of by a man."

"Benjamin has every reason to be proud of you."

Her grip on the chair eased. "Besides, you have other, more important things on your plate right now."

Sawyer edged around to her side of the table and propped his hip at the corner. Her skin didn't blanch and she didn't dart away. His outburst had pushed her. Hard. But she *was* standing on her own two feet. The woman was stronger than she gave herself credit for. "Nothing is more important than your family's safety."

"I know you feel things." She reached out and lightly touched the badge and black ribbon clipped to his belt. "I heard what Agent Holt said about your father. I'm sorry for your loss. You seemed so sensitive about it. Was it recent?"

"We buried him yesterday."

That crumbled the mask into dust, and he saw real compassion, real hurt on his behalf in her beautiful face. "Oh, Sawyer. And you're here with us when you should be with your own family? I am so sorry."

She raised her hand to touch his face, maybe to apologize, maybe to console him. But at the last second she hesitated and started to pull away. He grabbed her hand and pulled it back, spreading it flat over his heart, holding her close—needing the healing touch that some part of her wanted to give.

"Please don't be afraid of me."

"Intellectually—I'm not. I know you're not a monster. I've seen you with Benjamin and Mom. I know you tried to help me at the casino last year. And today." She shifted her stance and moved in half a step. Near enough that her thigh butted against his and her free hand rested on his arm. "But when you've breathed fear the same way most people breathe air, it's hard to always be rational. I've been punished for feeling things. Nearly killed for caring. So I'm, understandably, a little skittish about who I get close to. And you don't strike me as the most patient man I've ever met."

"I wouldn't say it's a strength of mine."

Her mouth curved with the beginnings of a smile. "You have other strengths. Like your dogged determination. The way you charm my mother and talk to Benjamin as though everything he says makes sense. You have a big heart." Her left hand came up to rest lightly beside the other, atop the quickening beat inside his chest. "I never knew my father. Tell me about yours."

He reached up to hold on to that small gift of warmth and caring.

"He was my dad. A cop with thirty years on the force. He taught my brothers and me how to be men. Taught a lot of others how to be good cops. He showed us how to love a woman by being so good to my mom. Well, she kind of trained *him* in that department." A soft laugh sounded in her throat and a sheen of tears glistened in her eyes, both touching the sorrow deep inside him.

He looked down to where their hands were joined together—hers, small and practical and pale compared to his big, tanned, work-roughened fingers. And yet he was the one feeling as though he needed to hold on to something. "It hurts to know he's gone. It pisses me off that someone could murder such a great man. But I can't do a damn thing about it because he *is* family. KCPD won't let me…won't let any of us in my family help. Departmental protocol. Prejudicing the D.A.'s case if they do catch somebody. They think we'd all be loose cannons, as if we didn't learn a damn thing from him."

She had to sense the anger and frustration and grief brewing inside him. Summoning every bit of his willpower, Sawyer eased his clasp on her so she could pull away.

But she didn't. Instead, she skimmed her fingers across the front of his shirt, stroking away the wrinkles, soothing away something hard and painful deep inside him. "It's still too fresh. It hurts too much. I'm sure they're trying to protect you and your family as much as they're protecting the investigation."

The petting stopped, and when she still didn't pull away, Sawyer let his hands settle at her waist. He kneaded his fingertips into the soft cotton of her sweater until he found the softer woman underneath. "I'm not much good to you right now, am I."

Her serene smile reached right down to his soul with a touch as warm and gentle as her hands had been. "Trust me. I understand about feeling helpless. About not being able to make things right for yourself or the people you love."

"How do you do it? How do you keep it from eating you up inside?"

"I work a lot. Go to school so I can get a better job. Stay busy. See my trauma counselor once a month. And I concentrate on raising Benjamin and supporting Mom. I try to be strong in every way I can be."

Taking a lesson from her gentle caresses, Sawyer brushed a wavy tendril off her forehead and tucked it behind her ear. With the pad of his thumb, he caught a tear that had spilled over and wiped it away. "Those are just distractions so you don't know how much it hurts."

"Maybe. But to me it means I'm moving forward with my life. It may be a slow journey, but moving forward gives me hope. Meanwhile, all those distractions give that wounded part inside a chance to heal."

He let his thumb drift down the velvet of her cheek, grazing ever so closely beside her scar of valor. "Okay, Dr. Mel—so is it all right if I concentrate on you and your family for a little while? Give that wounded part inside me a chance to heal?"

She didn't flinch, didn't pull away. He bowed his head, bringing his face closer to hers. He inhaled her sweet, clean fragrance, reveling in this quiet intimacy that felt so new yet seemed so right.

Her fingers curled beneath the collar of his shirt. "I can't make any promises. And I'm pretty sure my life's a little more screwed up than you realize—"

He erased the distance between them and

pressed his lips against hers in the gentlest kiss he knew how to give. For a moment, her breath caught, her fingers stilled. But then a warm sigh whispered across his skin, and her mouth softened and moved beneath his.

It was a chaste exploration, with only their lips and hands and denim-clad thighs touching each other. But with every press of his lips, she pressed back. With every gentle nip, she nibbled. With every needy moan in his throat, he heard an answering whimper from her. Melissa's kiss reached out to that wounded part inside him, pouring a balm over his grief.

But her winsome touch and earthy moans kindled a different kind of restlessness in the part of him that was hale and healthy and had always been half in love with her. She'd parted her lips and clutched a death grip on the front of his shirt. But when he followed his instincts, swept his tongue across the warm, supple seam and tried to deepen the kiss, she slipped her hand up between their chins, pushing him away while she retreated. "I'm sorry."

She had to have felt his heart pounding in his chest. "I'm not."

"Sawyer—"

"All right." He put his hands up in surrender, reining in his desire before he spoiled the precious moment that had just passed between them. "I'm sorry if I overstepped the bounds of friendship or did anything to jeopardize your trust in me."

"I'm a grown woman. You didn't do anything I didn't want you to."

So why did she look so upset by that kiss?

Wait a minute.

"You feel it, too, don't you. That…attraction between us?" She hugged her arms around her middle and he wished he could do that for her. Instead, he moved to the opposite side of the table and gave her the space she needed.

She wasn't afraid of *him*. She was afraid of *her* response to him.

Melissa faced him with a wry look on her face. "Okay, fine. Yes, there's something between us. And, yes, back when we were working at the Riverboat Casino, I might have indulged in a fantasy or two about you." He started to smile. It was nice to know he wasn't such a sap that he couldn't get his signals straight with a woman. But her next words killed any sense of victory. "But when I first met Ace, I thought I cared about him, too."

"I am not Ace Longbow."

"No. But do you think it's easy for me to trust my judgment again after a screwup like that?"

"I am *not* gonna let you down," he vowed. And then, before she could come up with some other argument to push him away, he pulled a card from behind his badge and tossed it onto the table. "Call me if you see anything suspicious, if anything spooks you—if your mom wants a ride to work or Benjamin wants me to come over and play. Anything."

Her shoulders sagged as she shook her head. "You've already done enough. You have your own family to think of."

He snatched up the stack of letters with one hand and palmed the back of her head with the other. And then he didn't think, didn't second-guess, didn't hesitate—he dipped his head and kissed her. He plunged his tongue inside her mouth and tasted the hint of coffee and a flavor that was uniquely her own that lingered there.

Sawyer kissed her like he meant business. And damn it, if the woman didn't kiss him back.

He kissed her hard. Kissed her quick.

And then he headed out the front door while he still had the strength to leave. "Call me."

Once he heard the three locks snap into place behind him, Sawyer stepped off the porch and climbed into his truck. But he only got a couple of blocks before he had to stop and pull over to let the upswell of raw emotions— grief, desire, rage at the man who could make such a sweet, gentle woman doubt she was anything but smart and strong and perfect—and something newer, deeper, and as powerful as anything he'd ever known—take him. He squeezed the steering wheel in his fists and cursed and cried as the feelings buffeted him from the inside out.

And when he was quiet again—when his eyes were dry and his energy spent and the only sound was the wiper blades sweeping back and forth across the windshield—he said a short, heartfelt prayer. "Sorry, Dad. Not much of a testament to how you raised me to lose it like that. Help me do better."

Doing better meant not allowing Longbow's legacy to shatter the fragile relationship budding between him and Melissa. Doing better meant getting his priorities straight and staying sharp and doing the job he'd been trained to do.

But the letters sitting in the seat beside him taunted his new resolve. Maybe it was a bit of morbid curiosity that made him pull the first envelope from the stack, but he justified opening the letter as being a diligent detective looking for clues that could protect a woman in trouble and help him catch a trio of killers.

It was dated the previous summer—about the time Mel was in the hospital, slowly rebuilding her body from the vicious beating that had put Ace in jail in the first place.

Little one,
    I miss you the way the prairie misses the rain and dries up to dust. I love you. Come see me as soon as you can. I know now that Mr. Wolfe means nothing to you. You have yourself and the kid to think of, so keeping your job is important to you, and that's why you were nice to him. I forgive you this time. As long as you come to see me.

He couldn't read on. Even the first few lines of what he read made him sick, expressing love and a threat in the very same paragraph.

Avoiding the urge to crumple the vile note in his fist, Sawyer carefully put it away. He'd read them all before he handed them over to Holt. But not tonight. Tonight he wanted to hold tight to the memory of something healing and sweet and wonderful that might never be his.

No wonder his father had come home or called every single night he'd been able. A man—a cop—needed something good in his life to sustain him through all the crap he had to deal with—like the pile of letters sitting beside him.

Before he slipped his truck back into gear, Sawyer pulled his phone from his pocket and speed dialed a familiar number.

"Hey, Mom? Yeah, it's me. Sorry to be calling so late. I just wanted to hear your voice and find out how you're doing."

MELISSA LAY AWAKE in the dark, listening to the rain beat against her window, as steady and relentless as the fears and doubts that toyed at the edges of her conscious mind.

She'd come so far since leaving Ace and filing for divorce. She'd survived her stay in the hospital. She'd mended her shattered bones and regained her strength. She'd earned a scholarship to help pay for the accounting degree she'd finish in another year and found a job at a respectable place that understood family schedules and paid a decent wage. She was raising a beautiful son and was lucky enough to have her best friend for a mother.

Once upon a time she'd had a rosy-eyed, fairy-tale vision for her future. Now she understood that her family's well-being, her health and a roof over her head were enough.

She rolled over in bed, snuggling with the body pillow that was almost as long as she was, feeling chilly and lonesome and oddly discontent. For the first time in months— maybe the first time in years—she wanted something more than to feel safe. She wished for something bigger than doing okay.

Tonight, for the first time since forever, she wanted to dream.

But sleep wouldn't come.

Sure, bed wasn't always an easy place to be, remembering the awful things that Ace had done to her in their marriage bed. But she blanked the images with a big red stop sign in her head, just as her therapist had taught her.

Melissa smiled into the pillow at a twisted, ironic thought. Ace probably wouldn't want her now, with the half-moon scar on her face.

But another man might.

Suddenly just as warm as she'd been

chilled a moment ago, Melissa pushed the pillow aside and rolled onto her back. She brushed her fingers over the puckered skin running from cheek to jaw, remembering with vivid clarity how gently, almost reverently, Sawyer had touched her there.

She thought about that kiss, too. The tender one that crept around her defenses and blended with her sympathy and instinct to offer comfort to ease Sawyer's pain. The sneaky part was that she'd found solace in that embrace as well.

And then there was the other kiss.

The needy one.

The one that had blown away memories of any other man. The one that had shown her what passion could be like—*should* be like. The one that was over and done with before she realized how whole and sexy and powerful she could be.

That's what she wanted to dream about.

She rolled over again to check the clock. 2:00 a.m. "Damn you, Sawyer Kincaid."

If he wasn't such a nice guy, she wouldn't even be considering the idea of kissing him again.

And she'd be sound asleep.

Giving up on the idea of resolving her need

for independence with her dream of having a normal, healthy relationship with a man, Melissa rolled out of bed, stepped into her slippers and walked out to the kitchen. If she couldn't get any sleep, she might as well be using her time to get something useful done.

She pulled her homework from her book bag and poured herself a glass of milk. As she set up her work space on the table, she noticed Sawyer's black leather jacket still hanging from the back of the chair where he'd sat to eat two slices of her mother's pie and ease her worries.

If Ace had left his jacket behind, he would have called her and accused her of forgetting to hand it to him. No, he would have stormed into the house and awakened her without apology. And if she was lucky, tossed the chair and not her across the room.

"Stop." Melissa threw up that big red stop sign and dismissed the image of violence from her mind.

She replaced it with a kinder, almost comical picture of a big man and little boy who barely reached his thigh debating the pluses and minuses of using a step stool rather than a Tonka truck to rehang the shades at her front windows.

Smiling at the silly memory of peeking around the corner to see a grown man being bested by four-year-old logic, Melissa touched the cool, supple leather of Sawyer's jacket. She curled her fingers into the buttery soft material, releasing the same scent that had clung to Sawyer himself. Smelling delicious and being good with kids were definitely nice-guy traits.

And losing herself so deeply so fast was a danger to her self-imposed promise to never allow a man to take over her life again.

Melissa pulled her hand away and sat down to her books and calculator.

She was halfway through her glass of milk when the telephone rang.

A line squiggled across her paper when she jerked. "Oh, God."

Her mind went to a dozen different places in the span of a second. Sawyer had remembered his jacket, didn't mind waking her family and wasn't so nice, after all. The authorities were calling to tell her they'd found Ace's body. Riley Holt was coming to arrest her for aiding and abetting an escaped felon. It was Ace himself. Or a damn wrong number.

Glad that Benjamin and her mother both slept soundly so that the panic was hers alone, Melissa scrambled to her feet and checked the caller ID. Recognizing the number as neither friend nor foe, and knowing someone else might wake if she let the phone continue to ring, Melissa took a deep breath and picked up.

"Hello?"

Silence. Long enough for her stomach to knot.

And then, "It's me, little one."

Ace.

Her knees turned to jelly and her blood ran cold. She couldn't speak.

"Baby?" He was in his sweetly contrite tone. The one that lied. The one that apologized after inflicting the pain. Melissa flattened her back against the wall and started to sink to the floor. "I need to see you. I'm hurt bad. I need your help."

She couldn't just hang up. Hanging up wouldn't make him go away. She swallowed hard and found her voice. "How did you get this number?"

Ace laughed. "I know you too well, baby. I knew where to look. Nothing can keep me from the woman I love."

"Where are you?" In Kansas City? Right down the block? *On my front porch?*

Melissa's legs suddenly turned to steel and she pushed herself away from the wall, hurrying as close to the front door as the phone cord would allow.

"Don't worry, little one. I know the feds are looking for me. I won't put you in danger by asking you to come to me. I'll come to you."

"No."

"I need some first aid, and I remember how gentle your hands are. You'll take good care of me, I know."

"No."

"I'll find you, little one. Sometime soon. When we can be alone. I love you."

"No!"

She slammed the phone back down on its cradle. She was breathing so fast and hard, it made her light-headed.

She had to think. Had to move. Had to do.

Seeking answers, her gaze landed on the small white business card still sitting on the table. She picked up Sawyer's number and ran back to the phone. But she hung up after punching in the fourth number.

She seized control of the panic and forced herself to breathe deeply, counting to five. Breathe in. Counting to five again. *Breathe out.*

It was so late and it was so easy to lean on someone strong like that. If she caved in now, she might never find the strength to take care of herself again.

She had to deal with this herself. She had to handle the fear on her own because Sawyer Kincaid wasn't always going to be around to take care of her. She wasn't weak. She wasn't stupid. She wasn't a victim.

And she refused to let Ace turn her into one again.

So Melissa tucked Sawyer's card into her sleeve and stooped down to unhook the phone from its jack so that Ace couldn't call her again. Then she ran from window to window, door to door, making sure everything was locked up tight. She peeked through the curtains to verify that Officer Cho was sitting in his police car and all was quiet outside.

She checked on her mother, made sure Benjamin was resting quietly, then brushed the hair off his forehead and leaned over the bed rail to kiss him. Then she hurried back to her own room and pulled her jeans on over her pajama pants before returning to the kitchen. She armed herself with the biggest butcher knife she could find and dragged a chair into the hallway between the two bedroom doors.

Independence was a good thing. Necessary to survive.

But a little boost of confidence never hurt anybody.

Melissa went back to the kitchen and put on Sawyer's jacket. She swam in its volume, but wrapped it around her like a warm, protective hug. She buried her nose in the collar, absorbing his scent, absorbing his strength.

And then Melissa sat in the chair with the knife and waited for morning—or death—to come.

Chapter Six

"Another dead body."

Sawyer stood at the edge of the early-morning crime scene, shining his flashlight down at the gray-haired black man wearing a three-piece suit and a spray of bullet holes across his chest. What the hell was happening to his city? Had some pervert developed a grudge against father figures?

He checked his watch. No way was he going to get out of here by 6:00 a.m. to drive Melissa to work. Hell, by the time the crime scene investigators arrived and he was finished canvassing the neighborhood for witnesses who were awake and willing to talk, he'd be lucky to be gone by lunch. He'd better call Officer Cho and ask him to do chauffeur duty.

At least it had stopped raining. But after so many days of the dreary stuff, he figured the predawn lull was just a teaser to make him think the sun might actually shine when it came up this morning.

"You say *dead body* like it's a bad thing." A lanky detective with chocolate skin, a tailored leather coat and as much gold bling as the department would let him wear walked out of the alley with a flashlight of his own, grinning around the toothpick he clutched between his teeth.

Sawyer laughed at the irreverent humor of a friend he hadn't seen in months. Joe Hendricks Jr. A second-generation cop, just like the Kincaid brothers. Much too stylish for a moniker as ordinary as Joe or Junior. "J.R. Aren't you in fine form this morning."

"I'm always in fine form, my friend. So what's your beef with my dead body?"

"It's just not the one I was hoping to find."

"Now, that's a cryptic statement."

"Long story." Sawyer ducked under the yellow crime scene tape and reached out to shake hands. "Good to see you, J.R."

"You too, Kincaid. Sorry to hear about your dad."

"Thanks."

"He was one of the good ones."

Sawyer nodded.

J.R. walked Sawyer over to the body and circled to the opposite side. "So what brings a Fourth Precinct detective down to my part of town?"

"Luck, I guess." J.R. wasn't the only cop with a sarcastic wit. "I came back right after Dad's funeral to help on the task force to recover those three fugitives from Jeff City."

The smell of garbage and drunks and standing water that wouldn't wash away blended with the coppery tang of the vic's blood. "Don't know if you noticed, but the murder of a retired brother in the middle of no-man's-land doesn't have anything to do with that task force."

"I noticed." Sawyer's deep exhale formed a cloud when it met the nip in the chilly air. "Captain Taylor thought this might be a 'more suitable' duty assignment for me."

"Shot your mouth off to the feds, eh?"

"Just the one. I don't like how he runs his investigation. Guess I'm not enough of a yes-man for him."

"You're not a yes-man to anybody, are you?"

"Nope." J.R. chastised his lame joke as Sawyer tugged up the thighs of his jeans and knelt beside the corpse. "So who do we have here?"

"According to his state ID card, he's James Cullen McBride, age sixty-two. Somebody's gone through his pockets—there's no cash on him and his watch is missing. But I have a feeling that happened after the fact—to make the murder look like a mugging. There are just too many bullets. And if it *was* a bash and grab, they'd have taken the whole wallet and not messed with cleanin' house."

"They'd have grabbed that bottle of pills, too." Sawyer pulled a pen from his chest pocket and used it to roll the brown plastic bottle on the concrete beside the body so he could read the label. "Digoxin. Isn't that heart medication? That's gotta have some street value."

"Tough way to go. Probably dying, anyway, and this had to happen."

Sawyer tilted his head up. "Is there any way this could be gang related?"

"The hood's right, but the victim's wrong. Gangstas don't usually target guys his age— unless it's a shopkeeper they're trying to rob, or someone tries to be the hero in a car jacking. Mr. McBride's carrying a bus pass instead of a license. I'm thinking he doesn't have a car to drive." That eliminated carjacking.

"And you don't recognize him as a local?"

J.R. squatted to match Sawyers's stance on the other side. He pulled the toothpick from the corner of his mouth and used it to point out the man's manicured nails. "He's not from around here. This guy's high-class money. Judging by all the blood, this is the kill scene, but something had to have lured him down here. Unless someone saw something and steps forward, it'll be up to the lab to piece together what happened to him."

"What are the chances of someone stepping forward?"

"In *this* neighborhood?" About as impossible as he'd expected. Sawyer and J.R. stood at the squeal of brakes on the damp pavement behind them. "There's the CSI team."

They both turned their lights on the tall, skinny brunette who clambered down from behind the wheel of the SUV. She grabbed her black lab case and haphazardly pulled her reflective orange vest on over her head as she marched across the sidewalk. Her arms and the vest got tangled up in the cordoning tape, but barely slowed her down. She freed herself before Sawyer could get over there to help and hurried right past him.

"I'm Holly Masterson, M.E." She nudged

J.R. aside before setting down her kit and casting accusing looks at both men. "Did you move my body?"

Her body?

"I went through his pockets to find his ID after the patrolmen called it in, ma'am," J.R. volunteered. "But the position of the body and items around him are just the way I found them."

"I turned over the bottle of pills with my pen to read the name," Sawyer added.

"Great," she fumed, propping her hands at her hips. "Just great."

The rest of Dr. Masterson's team was just now crawling beneath the tape. With the daggers she'd glared at Sawyer and J.R., it was little wonder the other CSIs weren't in a hurry to report for duty with her.

As she stooped down and went to work, J.R. sidled over to Sawyer and whispered, "Somebody's havin' a bad day."

Mood aside, there was nothing wrong with the lady doctor's hearing. "I'm having a bad year, Detective." With a flick of her hand she shooed them away. "Go about your duties, Officers, and let my team get their work done here before we pollute the scene any more."

"We usually leave her in the lab," one of the techs muttered as he passed by. "She's filling in."

"That's enough, Rick." Holly Masterson turned on her own light to work by, and Sawyer could see by the lines on her face that she was frazzled, fatigued and way too stressed to be reasoned with right now. "Why don't you walk the perimeter—see if you can find shell casings to go with at least four entry wounds."

"I'm on it already."

"Gentlemen?" Sawyer and J.R. both understood *that* look, and wisely moved to the other side of the crime scene tape to give Dr. Masterson her space.

"So...you want to wake people up or wait until daylight?" J.R. asked. Sawyer headed for the first apartment.

They'd roused nearly an entire building of tenants who may or may not have heard gunshots, when Sawyer's cell phone buzzed on his belt. When he read the caller ID, he motioned J.R. to wait, and snapped open his phone.

"Mel?" He'd hoped. But he hadn't really expected her to call. He shouldn't be feeling this adolescent rush of euphoria. Ah, hell.

He shouldn't be feeling anything but worry. "What's up?"

"He has my phone number." No need to explain who *he* was.

Adolescence vanished. Cop kicked in.

"Ace called?" Galvanized by the bombardment of worst-case scenarios that instantly filled his head, Sawyer took the stairs down to the lobby three at a time.

"I think he broke into the shop where Mom works and got it." He'd take that as a yes. Her tone was a little too soft, her articulation stretched a little too tight. "There were break-ins at three sporting goods stores last night. It's on the news."

Were those TV voices he heard in the background? Or was she at a precinct office? Sawyer was already jogging toward his truck. "If he has your phone number, then—"

"He knows where I live."

Not good. Not good at all. "Is everybody okay? Is Cho there with you?"

"Yo, Kincaid—where you runnin'?" J.R. easily caught up to him and snagged the sleeve of Sawyer's tweed jacket. His dark eyes narrowed with curiosity and concern. "Is there a fire somewhere?"

Sawyer turned the phone away from his

ear for just a second, hating that he was this far away from Melissa when Longbow had gotten so close. "Something personal's come up I need to take care of."

"On your dad's case?"

"No, it's…it's—"

"Important." J.R. held the door when Sawyer swung it open and climbed inside his truck. "Go."

Sawyer nodded toward the lights set up around James McBride's body and the techs still processing the scene. "I'm sorry to bail. Have you got this under control?"

J.R. nodded, obviously sensing the need if not understanding the situation. "I'll copy you on my report. Get out of here."

"I owe you one."

"I know."

Sawyer hit the headlights and jammed the truck into gear. "Mel?" He wedged the phone between his shoulder and ear and zigzagged through the maze of vehicles at the murder site. "You still there? I'm on my way."

"I'm at Pearl's Diner with Benjamin. I brought him with me and sent Mom to a friend's house. She was pretty shaken up when I told her. I think she feels responsible. I told her I don't blame her."

"You went to work?" That explained the background noise. But not the risk. "Put Cho on the line."

"He's not here. When I went out to the car this morning, Officer Cho was gone."

Mentally, Sawyer took back every nice thing he'd said about the kid and stepped on the gas. "He was supposed to stay with you until eight."

"There were three other cars there. One in the driveway, two in the street. With men I don't know inside. Wearing suits. One of them followed us into the city. Another one followed Mom. I guess the third's still at the house."

Strangers, not Ace. Still not good.

"They're probably Holt's men. I'll call to verify."

"Agent Holt's here at the diner. Sawyer?" He took a corner a little too fast and a lot too wide at the hitch he heard in her voice.

"Mel?"

"He's using me for bait. He knows Ace wants to see me. His men are everywhere. In the diner. Up and down the street. There are reporters here, too. At least he's keeping them away from Benjamin, but… I thought I'd be safer if we were surrounded by people we knew. But…it's crazy here."

I'm scared.

He could hear it in her voice. For a woman who'd fought so hard to regain control of her life, having Holt's armed circus move in must feel like having her feet kicked out from under her.

Sawyer's hands fisted on the wheel. That smug son of a bitch. If Melissa got hurt— even killed—it wouldn't matter to Golden Boy just so long as he captured his man.

But it mattered one hell of a lot to Sawyer.

"Don't you leave that diner. I'm on my way."

"No, no, sweetie." Melissa set down the plate she was carrying and guided Benjamin around to the stools on the other side of the counter. "I need you to stay out front with Pearl. There are too many hot things and sharp utensils back here. Up you go." She boosted him onto her hip and lifted him back to his perch on the stool.

"There's my baby boy." Pearl Jenkins waddled up to the stool next to Benjamin and placed a box of crayons in front of him.

"I'm a *big* boy," Benjamin insisted, cracking open the box and evaluating his choices.

Pearl chuckled. "That you are, my dear. That you are. I'm sorry I lost track of him for a minute, Melissa. I had to check out the customers up front. I'll make sure someone has their eye on him next time."

Pearl's roly-poly figure was due to a lifetime of fabulous home-style cooking, and the lines behind her glasses were due to laughter as much as the stress of running her own business. It was the stress part Melissa worried about this morning. "I'm the one who's sorry, Pearl. I know it's not professional to dump Ben on you like this. And all these extra people and the TV cameras out front keeping your regulars, like the construction workers across the street, from finding a spot for breakfast? I should have thought this through better."

"Don't be silly." She squeezed Melissa's hand. "Look at all the free advertising I'm getting. Some of those curiosity seekers gathering outside might become new customers, and I'm making every last one of Agent Holt's men buy the coffee they're drinking."

Melissa felt her first real smile of the morning coming on. Pearl might be big-hearted and generous to a fault, but she was a shrewd businesswoman through and through. "Still, I shouldn't have stuck you with baby-sitting duty with all this chaos going on."

Pearl cleared her throat with a conspiratorial tone and pointed to Benjamin and the pies—or possibly spaceships—he was drawing. "Who's babysitting? I'm watching the big boy here. My grandkids are all in California now, so this is a treat. Besides, with those men on the loose, I want you and your son someplace safe." She nodded to the plate on the counter. "I don't serve cold food here. You'd better get that out to the table."

"Thanks, Pearl."

Her employer was already asking Ben about his picture, acting as though giving them refuge this morning was no big deal. Silently, Melissa promised that once she got her accounting degree, she'd do Pearl's taxes for free, or manage her books—or give whatever gift she could to show her gratitude.

In the meantime, the plate was cooling, and their customers were hungry. Balancing the second dish on her forearm, she picked up a pot of coffee and hurried out to the tables.

It was impossible to keep her eyes on her destination, though, when booth after booth she passed held one or more agents. They were all dressed in a variety of civilian clothes—a man in work jeans there, a man and woman looking like any yuppie couple—sipping coffee, pushing food around their plates. But the curling cords running down the back of their necks and the alert, watchful gazes monitoring the crowd inside the diner and outside on the street gave them away.

Agent Holt had instructed her to treat them like any other customer—exchange polite, impersonal chitchat, take their orders, serve their food—so that nothing would seem out of place and possibly scare Ace away should he try to reach her here.

But everything felt out of place this morning. Benjamin was here, endearing himself to all the staff and sometimes getting underfoot, instead of sleeping in at home with her mother. Holt was reluctantly staging a press conference on the sidewalk out front. It seemed to require every ounce of patience not to snap at the reporters asking for updates on the manhunt. Plus the lights from television crews and camera flashes gave the air an eerie glow. The bell over the door jangled against her nerves as customers came and went, determined to eat, maybe to catch a glimpse of a real FBI agent or just to walk through the camera shot and get their ten seconds of fame.

Melissa dropped off the plates and made

rounds at her tables with the coffee. Though she could normally wait tables in her sleep, it was difficult to concentrate on her duties when she knew the commotion on the other side of that long plate-glass window was all because of her presence here.

"I'll find you, little one... Nothing can keep me away."

She filled a teacup with coffee by mistake, and had to replace it.

"I'm on my way."

She crossed to the window and looked out into the crowd. Funny how two men, with two similar messages, could make her feel so completely different. One promise destroyed. The other empowered.

"Where are you, Sawyer?" she whispered. She spread her fingers against the cool pane and squinted past the artificial lights to scan the faces, one by one.

The sun had risen, turning the sky a lighter shade of gray as a mist that wasn't quite yet rain filled the air. Not that a sudden downpour would chase anyone away, judging by the rapt interest of the group milling around in the street and the construction workers gathering across the way instead of going inside the old brick building they were remodeling into apartments. "Where are you?"

Even her growing connection to the big cop with the boyish grin seemed out of place in the ordered, predictable life she'd tried to build for herself and her family. Whatever she was feeling for Sawyer Kincaid was seeping through the chinks in her protective armor and turning into something much bigger and more frightening than she'd imagined she was even capable of feeling anymore.

She could stand up to her own fears in the middle of the night. She could defend her family from the nightmare she'd brought into their lives when she'd married Ace at nineteen. But she wasn't sure she had it in her to do that *and* stand up to a team of federal agents sweeping into her home and bugging her phone, setting up cameras to watch her yard from a neighboring house, dismissing Cho, questioning her mother, frightening her son—

"Miss?"

"What?" She turned, startled. An expectant customer was holding up his coffee mug. But the cup was already full. "I'm sorry?"

"I asked if I could get some cream?"

"Of course. I'll bring it right out." She hurried back behind the counter, hating this disappointment she felt.

Sawyer couldn't get to her through this zoo. She should take heart in the notion that that meant Ace probably couldn't get to her, either. But she'd felt so much better when she finally heard Sawyer's voice on the phone. Even better than his warm, cushy jacket, his deep, urgent—caring—voice had calmed her, reassured her, strengthened her.

But she shouldn't have put so much stock in him making the insanity go away this morning. He meant well. He really did. But she needed to go back to that place she'd been before he'd ever barged into her life and given her hope. Back to when she was self-reliant. Back to when she could count on never being let down by a broken promise again.

Sparing a smile and a tweak for Benjamin, Melissa carried the pitcher of half-and-half out to the table. "Here you go."

"Thanks."

She felt him. A sixth sense crawling up her spine and turning her blood to ice. Melissa made herself turn to the window.

Oh. My. God.

Looking right at her. Sunglasses on a rainy day. A flash of movement in the back at the crowd and he was gone.

Ace. She dashed to the window. "No."

She scanned the people outside, looking from face to face. Looking for height. Looking for…was it a hat? A hood? His skin was whiter, as if he wore makeup. How did a big man get lost so quickly? She clutched at the glass that gave her no purchase. "Where did you go?"

"Ma'am?" One of the agents tried to get her attention. "Did you see something?"

"I'm not crazy." Not what he'd asked, but she ran for the door, determined to prove that to herself.

How many times in the beginning had she tried to reach out for help, only to discover how well Ace had isolated her from the world so that no one believed her suffering? How many times had she been fool enough to dismiss her fear because he'd been so remorseful or had started some kind of counseling? How many times had she tried to predict the mood swings and live with the danger? Or stand up to him and pay a very dear price?

How many times had Ace called her crazy for even considering that he didn't really love her?

"You don't get to win this time, Ace." She darted around the line waiting to be seated and pushed open the front door. A spotlight blinded her eyes and the chilly mist hit her face, freezing her into place. But only for a moment.

She blinked her vision clear and stretched up on tiptoe, wishing she was a foot taller. She ran down the sidewalk, searching wherever there was a break in the crowd. Was that him behind the umbrella? Carrying the ladder inside the archway across the street?

She circled behind Holt and a female reporter, squeezing past a line of print journalists holding notepads and tape recorders. What about the man ducking his head against the moist air and hurrying down the sidewalk? Had an agent spotted him and picked him up already?

The first solid drop of rain plopped against her cheek and she shook it off. Was it *him*? Or *that* man?

"We need to wrap this up and clear the street." Riley Holt's clear, concise voice carried over the murmur of complaints about the rain starting up again. "The body found inside the Sports Emporium has been identified as Henry Brennerman. We can now confirm that Richard Longbow also survived the escape attempt. He remains at large, though we believe he is seriously injured. We have every hospital in the nine-state area on alert for anyone matching his description. We continue to consider him and Tyrell Mayweather extremely dangerous."

"Can you confirm Mayweather's...?"

Melissa jumped as the crowd closed ranks in an effort to stay dry. "No, please. I'm trying to see."

"Sir?"

"Agent Holt?"

His men had followed her out.

"Excuse me." There was a disrupting whir of clicks and flashes as Agent Holt abruptly ended the interview. "We're done. Please remind viewers of our tip-line number."

"Thank you, Agent Holt. This is Hayley Resnick, Channel Four Eyewitness News. Now back to Ken in the weather center for more updates on those flash-flood warnings."

"Miss Teague?" She gasped at the hand on her arm, and scratched at it as he whirled around. "Easy." Riley Holt snatched her other wrist and pulled her fingernails away before she realized she was attacking a federal officer and stopped herself. "What are you doing out here by yourself?"

For an instant, her heart had stopped. Now

it was racing. "I saw him. Ace was here, watching me through the window."

"Shh. We don't want to cause a panic." He snapped his fingers above her head, and with hand signals dispersed his men to search. "Where did he go?"

"I can't find him now."

The crowd jostled her as the cameras shut down and interest waned. Holt pulled her closer to be heard over the chatter of conversations starting around them. "Look at all these people. Are you sure you didn't just imagine seeing him?"

"No!" She tugged against his grip, suddenly feeling like a captured fugitive herself. "Ace follows his own set of rules when it comes to me. A crowd won't stop him."

"Fine. Was Mayweather with him? What was he wearing?"

"Sunglasses. Some kind of disguise."

"Such as?"

"His hair was covered…" A gap opened between Melissa and the street and she craned her neck, desperate to find her ex before he disappeared and could haunt her without recourse again.

"I'm talking to you!"

"Ow!"

The agent's grip pinched as he jerked her attention back to him. She cringed at the don't-mess-with-me tone in his voice. "I need details, Miss—"

"Holt! Get your hands off her."

No. *That* was what *don't mess with me* sounded like.

"Sawyer?"

Striding through the crowd, his broad shoulders cleared a path.

Despite every vow of independence she'd tried to hold herself to just moments ago, an unabashed sense of relief swept over Melissa like the cooling rain. Holt released her and she ran straight into Sawyer's arms.

She didn't question the impulse, didn't doubt one step. She wound her arms beneath the nubby tweed of his jacket and latched on tight to the back of his belt. She aligned her body with his and turned her nose into the warmth and hardness of his chest. Her eyes were dry, but she was shaking from surviving another terrifying encounter with Ace.

"Are you okay?"

She clutched tighter. "I will be."

He dipped his lips to the crown of her hair and curved his shoulders around her. One long arm wrapped her up like a cocoon, shielding her from the outside world. His other hand gently cradled her scarred cheek. "You scared me."

Melissa burrowed into his heat, vaguely aware of Agent Holt speaking into a microphone on his wrist, giving orders to his men. "Fan out…radius. Floor by floor… I want a report in ten." There was a pause. "Miss Teague, if you can give me anything more to go on?"

"What's he talking about, Mel?"

Sawyer blocked out the rain, onlookers and the fuming federal agent—but even his gentle strength couldn't make her forget. "Ace was here. Watching me. I don't know where he went."

"Here!" Suddenly, they were moving.

"You're sure it was Longbow?" Agent Holt demanded.

"She's sure." He snugged her to his side, shielding her with his arm, half lifting her to match her pace to his longer stride as he steered her inside the diner to relative safety.

"Damn it, Kincaid, she has information I need."

"Damn yourself, Holt." The bell jangled over the opening and closing of the door like the beginning of a boxing match. Sawyer secured Melissa's hand in his and turned on Holt, who'd followed them in. "Even if you're low enough to use Mel as a decoy to lure Longbow in, any man with a badge should have sense enough to pull her out of a crowd like that."

"It was those damn reporters. But I had the situation under control. The crowd was dispersing. I don't know how she got away from my men. As soon as I saw her, I went after her myself."

"Mommy?" Oh, no. Benjamin stood up on the stool where he'd been drawing. His eyes were wide with concern.

"It's okay, sweetie." She motioned him to sit back down, and nodded to Pearl to help him to a less dangerous perch.

Sawyer was a millimeter away from poking his finger in the center of Agent Holt's chest. "You didn't have control of anything out there. You were milking the spotlight."

"I get results when I do my job, Kincaid. I don't have to explain myself to you."

"Too loud!" Benjamin had his hands over his ears now, clearly picking up on everyone's stress.

"Sawyer?" She wanted him to retreat.

The customers inside were becoming

every bit as interested in this exchange as they'd been in the interview outside. Melissa felt herself shrinking as, one by one, every muscle began to tense. She'd seen confrontations like this before with Ace. Two lions establishing dominance. And she was caught in the middle.

She curled her fingers into the sleeve of Sawyer's jacket. "Please—"

"I see your men creepin' up back there."

Melissa jerked her head to find two of Holt's men flanking them. "Stop this," she whispered, not loud enough for anyone to hear. "Benjamin is watching."

Holt raised one hand and the men halted their advance. But it wasn't a concession to her discomfort. It was a macho stance to show Sawyer the agent didn't need any help in dealing with him. "He said he'd come to her. Do you understand? Longbow wants to come out of hiding. The minute he does, he's mine. So trust me, we've had eyes on Miss Teague 24/7. She wasn't in any danger."

"Bull. Longbow could have abducted her, attacked her or worse, and you wouldn't know it until it was too late. Then you'd be out your fugitive *and* the means to find him."

Melissa's grip tightened. Her breathing

grew shallow. *No. Don't cave, girl. Stand on your own two feet.* She threw up a red stop sign on an image of Sawyer throwing a punch at Agent Holt. What if it went that far? *Stop!*

"Aren't you both on the same side? You should work together…" Too soft. Be strong.

Holt fired back. "You are off this case, Kincaid, do you hear me? Grieving or not, if you interfere one more time, I will have your badge."

And then she saw Benjamin climbing off his stool, running to her. "Stop being loud!"

"You leave my father's murder out—"

"Stop it!" Melissa scooped Benjamin up in her arms and hugged him tight. His trembling fed some maternal strength in her that gave her the backbone to take control of the entire room. "You two need to stop this feud and start working together. I am fine. But I'm not going to help either one of you if you frighten my little boy again."

There was a beat of silence that echoed all the way back into the kitchen. An interminable pause while the world rushed in on Melissa. Everyone in the diner heard her.

But one person listened.

"I'm sorry." Sawyer reached over and

tangled his fingers in Benjamin's hair. "I'm sorry, Big Ben. I didn't mean to scare you. Maybe I was just a little scared myself—about your mom." His gaze moved to Melissa's eyes, silently asking forgiveness. But he had a reassuring smile for Ben when he turned his head on her shoulder, sniffled, and decided he'd listen to Sawyer's apology. "Your mom's okay. You're okay, too."

With a deep breath, Sawyer turned back to the agent. His voice was deep. Calm. "I'm done arguing with you, Holt. Melissa's right—Longbow's the enemy here, not you. You do your job and I'll do mine."

"Your job doesn't include—"

"'Tawyer?" Benjamin, deciding he was pleased to see his big buddy, after all, stretched out his arms, demanding to be held.

"Benjamin, no."

But then he tried to scramble to the floor, and with a silent request for permission that she couldn't deny her son, Sawyer lifted Benjamin from her arms. "I've got you." His tone lightened from die-hard defender to pre-school playmate as he spoke. "Hey, Big Ben. Have you had breakfast yet?"

"I ate cereal," he announced proudly, paying no mind to Holt's silent red face.

"Is that all?" Sawyer teased. "What about the second half?"

"Second half of what?"

"The hot part of breakfast. We're good eaters, remember?" Melissa tagged along as Sawyer carried Ben toward an empty booth. "Do you like pancakes, Ben?"

He clapped his hands. "With mapa' syrup."

Holt followed, too, clearly suspicious of the sudden truce. "What are you up to, Kincaid?"

"Almost six-five when I stand up straight."

"You ass—"

"Hey!" Melissa cut Holt off and pointed a finger at him. "I don't like my son to hear that kind of language."

"What?" He seemed surprised that she'd stood up to him. Again. And, while the rest of the customers returned to their own business, perhaps assuming *she* had the situation under control now, Holt seemed to be reconsidering his damn-the-consequences approach to dealing with her. "I'm sorry. I wasn't thinking about the boy."

She could get used to standing on her own two feet—*and* feeling emotion. Pride. Maternal love. Victory.

Sawyer smiled down at her. "Is this booth in your section, miss?"

Melissa rediscovered some unfamiliar muscles and smiled back. "Yes, sir. Coffee's fresh. Menus are on the table. What can I get you?"

Sawyer set Ben on the seat and slid in beside him. "We'll skip the coffee and have two orders of pancakes with plenty of maple syrup, and two glasses of milk." He smiled down at Benjamin. "Sound good, buddy?"

"Tounds good."

Seeing how secure and calm Benjamin was around Sawyer, Melissa pulled out her pad and played the charade right along with them. "I'll get your order put right in, sirs."

Holt still hadn't conceded his authority on the investigation. "I told you you were off this investigation, Kincaid. My men have not only this building, but also this entire block, covered."

Sawyer accepted the crayon Benjamin handed him. "I'm on leave from the department this week, Agent Holt. I'm not investigating anything right now."

"So, what, you're gonna play bodyguard?"

Sawyer's grin matched Benjamin's. "I'm just here to eat breakfast with my friend Ben."

Riley Holt appeared to be swallowing a

bitter pill. "And I suppose this breakfast will take you the duration of Miss Teague's entire shift?"

Sawyer shrugged with fake innocence. "We *are* good eaters."

Ben piped in, apparently unaware of the tension between the two men now that Sawyer was taking a less confrontational approach. "That's how come we're so big."

"I can see that." Interesting. So Holt actually did know how to smile. But Melissa noted how quickly that smile vanished when he turned from Benjamin to Sawyer. "Eat up. Run interference between your girlfriend and me. But if Longbow shows his face again, and you get in my way when I move to capture him…"

Sawyer was done smiling, too. "I won't let Longbow hurt Melissa. I won't let you hurt her, either."

Chapter Seven

"Fritzi?" Susan Kincaid pushed open the kitchen's swinging door, carrying four thick books in her arms. "I actually found what I was looking for. My William Chrisman High School yearbooks."

Sawyer caught Fritzi's dish towel before it slipped off the counter. She was already hurrying across the kitchen. "A *Gleam?* Oh my goodness. I haven't seen one of those in forever. I lost mine in one of our moves. What years are they?"

He couldn't tell which woman was more pleased to have discovered a new friend tonight. They were both going through difficult times right now, yet both moms were as animated as he'd seen them in days.

After the day they'd had at the diner—staying one step ahead of Rick Holt and his lame plan to entrap Longbow—Sawyer had bundled up the Teagues and brought them home to his mother's house for dinner. He'd hoped showing Melissa, Fritzi and Benjamin what passed for pretty normal family life would give them a break from the lurking terror and life under a microscope that awaited them back home in Independence. Plus, spending time with him here would ease Melissa into the idea that he intended to stick around once he'd retrieved his jacket from her kitchen.

But who knew there'd be a bonus?

"Why don't you come out to the dining-room table and we'll have a look," Susan offered. "I know we graduated high school a few years apart, but since we share the same alma mater, I'm sure we'll find someone in common we both know."

Fritzi glanced back over her shoulder. "Well, Melissa and I were going to work on the dishes."

"Nonsense. That's what I had four sons for." Susan winked at Sawyer. "You don't mind taking over, do you, son?"

Oh, yeah, his mother was smiling. No way was he killing this mood. "You two go and enjoy your trip down memory lane. Mel and I have this covered." He dropped his gaze to

Melissa standing beside him at the sink. "Sorry, I didn't mean to volunteer you."

She pushed up her sleeves and dipped her hands into the suds. "Go on, Mom. You deserve a break. I think Holden's met his match playing Candy Land. So we won't have to worry about Benjamin for a while. Besides, I'd like some time alone with Sawyer."

Could their moms have scurried out of the kitchen any faster? And why did Melissa's last comment sound more ominous than seductive?

"I know what you're going to say." Sawyer might as well meet her well-rehearsed arguments head-on. "If I have to sleep in my truck out in the driveway, I am staying the night at your place."

"No, you're not," she stated just as firmly. She rinsed a pan and set it in the drainer. "And this has nothing to do with explaining a man staying over to Ben or Mom. I'm learning how to be more assertive, Sawyer. I…liked…standing up to Agent Holt—and you—at the diner. I'm still getting used to the idea that I can have an opinion and there won't be consequences. I don't want to back-track and become dependent on a man again."

"Being smart about keeping your family

safe is hardly the same thing as being terrorized into submission by Ace."

"I know, I know." She raised a drippy hand to placate him unnecessarily. "Don't think I'm ungrateful. I loved that you were there for me this morning, and it's been fun hanging out with you today. I know Benjamin has had a glorious time—with all this rain, he's been cooped up—"

"And your mom likes me, too. I know. I got this same thank-you speech last night." He dried the pan and set it on the stove. "I admire your quest for independence, but the stakes have escalated, sweetheart. Ace has made contact with you twice, and promises to do it again. And it's going to be more than a look or a phone call. I read those letters before I gave them to Holt." Her hands stilled in the water and she bowed her head so that he couldn't read her expression, not even reflected in the window over the sink. Sawyer's heart seemed to go pretty still, too. "I hope you're angry, not ashamed. Those weren't love letters. But I think Holt was right in that they give a pretty good idea of what Ace is like, what he's capable of."

"It's because of my weakness that he became so obsessed in the first place. He could use that to control me. I can't be that same person again. I can't give him that advantage."

"Being afraid of him only gives him an advantage if you let it. It's normal to have the feelings, remember? But I'm not automatically a bad guy if I lose my temper, and being afraid doesn't mean you're not still the toughest woman I know." He reached over and brushed a wheaten tendril off her face, exposing her scarred cheek. "You're not surrendering any hard-won independence by accepting some help to stand up to that bastard."

And then he dipped his head and gently kissed the mark. Her breath hitched. But she didn't pull away.

Sawyer's voice cracked with a husky whisper at the tenuous acceptance of his caring. "Ace risked being a part of that mob this morning, just to see you. I think he'd charge straight through Holt's defenses if he thought that was the only way he could get to you. And where do you think you'll be when those bullets start flying?"

At last she turned. Her face was close to his, her eyes studying his mouth as if analyzing the words that had just come out.

Her voice was hushed, like his. "There are

half a dozen federal agents stationed around my house. At least two more parked out in front of your mother's house right now."

"Holt's men are interested in Longbow. Not you." He tucked that same golden strand behind her ear. "I have a hard time with you—Ben and Fritzi, too—being a detail that gets overlooked. Ben's already growing up without a dad. I couldn't handle it if he had to grow up without a mother, too."

She reached up and touched his face with her wet hand, stroking his jaw. "It's for Benjamin's sake that I'm trying to be this strong. You saw how upset he got this morning at the diner. He needs to know that I can take care of us."

"My mom and dad were always stronger together."

Her tremulous smile cut straight to his heart. She brushed her fingertips across his lips and Sawyer didn't mind the taste of soap or the drips on his shirt. "I don't know what that's like, Sawyer."

"Let me show you. Let's be that team."

But the doorbell rang, and the sudden flurry of activity from other parts of the house broke the spell. He heard Holden's "We got it, Mom" calling from the family room. Melissa pulled away before he could reach her with either his logic or his love.

Sawyer straightened. Whoa. Love? He'd known the feelings were there for Melissa. He'd known they hadn't lessened any over the past few months. But when had he gotten tired of burying them inside and actually let them grow so strong? He supposed the past few days had stripped him of those filters that allowed him to pretend that need was nothing more than physical attraction, that something soul deep had disguised itself as friendship, and that love was just a bad case of doin' the right thing by her.

The kitchen door swung open and a parade entered. First came Holden, hauling Benjamin on his back. Then Fritzi. Then Susan Kincaid, with her arm linked through William Caldwell's.

"Bill." Sawyer stepped forward to shake hands with his father's friend. He shoved one of those emotional filters back into place and pretended that admitting the depth of what he felt for Melissa Teague hadn't just knocked him off his game. "This is a nice surprise."

But from the deep lines bracketing Bill Caldwell's tight mouth, he could see there was nothing *nice* behind this surprise.

"Sawyer." He shook Holden's hand, and Benjamin's, too. The rest of the introductions were made and then Bill leaned in and kissed Susan's cheek, apologizing. "I'm sorry for calling so late, Su. But I'm actually here to see Sawyer and Holden."

Susan squeezed his arm and nodded. "I think that means police business, ladies. Come on. Let's have Benjamin show us how to play that game."

Though she was still a little pale and a little too quiet for his peace of mind, Melissa scooped Benjamin off Holden's back and carried him out the door with the others.

Sawyer tossed his towel onto the counter and leaned back against it. Holden, looking the very image of their father when he stood like that, with his arms folded across his chest and that tiny furrow of concentration dimpling the center of his forehead, started the conversation. "What's up, Bill? Did you find out something on Dad's case?"

"I don't know. I'm not sure." He turned the brim of his damp felt hat between his hands. But then he breathed deeply, stopped fiddling with the hat and looked straight at Sawyer. "Is it true that James McBride was found dead this morning?"

Okay. Not what he was expecting. "Yeah, I worked the crime scene. I'll probably be assigned to it when I get back to work full-time. J. R. Hendricks is running the case for now, though. Why?"

"James McBride worked for me as an account manager. Before he retired. Heart problems, if I remember correctly. Too much stress, I'm sure." Though his speech had settled into the more confident cadence they were used to, Bill Caldwell's posture never relaxed. "I know you boys aren't officially working the investigation into your father's murder. But I also know that cops hear things. About other cases. I was wondering if maybe you've heard something that KCPD's trying to keep hush-hush?"

Holden frowned. "You mean about Dad's murder, or this McBride guy?"

"Sawyer, Holden..." Bill took a deep breath. "James McBride knew your dad, too. I remember John running into the two of us at a lunch meeting on the Plaza one day, and it was like old home week. They said they'd served in the army together. Must have been after my time in uniform because I didn't know McBride until I hired him to work for me years later. But they were more than passing acquaintances. And now they're both dead."

Sawyer stood away from the counter. "You think the two murders are connected?"

"I don't know." Bill was neither father figure nor CEO right now. He suddenly looked ashen, like a frightened old man. "Counting your father's death, James is the third old friend of mine who's died this year. We all knew each other—we're connected somehow. The first two deaths were from natural causes, but these last two have been under mysterious circumstances. Seems like I'm seeing a pattern here. I don't have that many old friends left.

"Should I be worried that I might be next?"

"ARE YOU SURE they can't see inside the house?" Fritzi shifted the umbrella to keep Sawyer's shoulder covered as he carried a sleeping Benjamin up onto the porch.

"Not unless you open the curtains." Sawyer looked behind him, sparing a glance for the two federal agents sitting in the car across the street. "But I guarantee you Holt has every inch of the yard and exterior of this house, as well as the neighbors' on each side, under surveillance."

Melissa pulled her key from the last lock and reached inside to turn on the porch light. It stayed on long enough to see the rivulets of water running down the siding between the porch roof and main house before the light shorted out and plunged them into darkness again. "Shoot. There's another repair that's not in my budget."

"Looks like it's just the lamp itself. Make sure you've got power inside." No electricity meant they were turning right around and climbing back into his truck. If he had to cram all three into his apartment or pay for hotel rooms, they wouldn't be staying here without electricity. They were already vulnerable enough without being able to follow weather reports or turn on security lights.

Melissa tried another switch and the hallway flooded with light. "Thank goodness."

There went another excuse to whisk this family away to a safer location Ace Longbow couldn't find. "Let's get in."

Instead of moving, Melissa blocked his path and held out her arms. "I can take Benjamin now. He must be getting heavy."

Territorial-mom urge? Or *her* attempt to get rid of him one last time?

"You're kidding, right? Just hold the

door—I've got him." The boy had zonked out almost as soon as Sawyer had started the engine on his truck and pulled out of his mother's driveway to take them all home. But even draped over his shoulder as dead weight, his little buddy didn't weigh as much as a sack of potatoes.

With a reluctant nod, Melissa opened the door the rest of the way. "His room's down the hall on the right. Mom? Will you lock the doors?" She reached up and touched Benjamin's raven-dark hair, then backed up. "This way."

In little more than forty-eight hours, Sawyer had learned what his father must have known all along about being a dad. It was a cool job—and Sawyer was quickly becoming addicted to it. Even if it would have strained every muscle in his body to carry him, Melissa's son would be a welcome burden. The boy had an unquestioning trust in Sawyer, and was free in sharing his thoughts and affection, as well as sharing his displeasure when he didn't get his way. Could Benjamin's mother ever learn to have that same kind of faith in him?

Sawyer followed Melissa down the hall to the tiny bedroom Benjamin shared with his grandmother. When she turned on the night-light, he could see the pair of twin beds. "I assume the one with the bed rail belongs to this guy?"

Melissa nodded. "Wait a sec." Working quickly and efficiently, she pulled off Benjamin's shoes, then unhooked the straps of his overalls and, with Sawyer's help, took them off. She pulled back the covers and Sawyer deposited his little charge onto the bed and stepped back to watch Melissa tuck him in and kiss him good night.

Sawyer didn't know if it was the smell of little boy clinging to his shirt, or the heartfelt mother's prayer Melissa whispered that left him standing in the middle of the room, tight-lipped and telling himself the rain had gotten into his eyes.

It was the gentle clutch of Melissa's hand around his that finally jarred him into moving again. "Sawyer?"

"I was thinking about my dad."

Her hand squeezed tighter. "Would you like to kiss Benjamin good night?"

Yeah. He'd like that.

"Go ahead. He won't bite."

It took a little nudge before he moved forward and knelt beside the bed. The soft light in the room gave Benjamin's innocent features an ethereal glow. Sawyer touched the tiny hand that barely filled his palm.

So this was the antidote for grief. A gentle woman and a precious little boy.

A knot untied itself around Sawyer's heart and something deeper, and more determined than ever to prevail, took root inside him.

He brushed the shock of hair off Benjamin's forehead and leaned over to press a kiss there. "'Night, Big Ben."

He bade Fritzi good night with a kiss on the cheek, adding supportive moms and good cooking to the list of things that made him feel more human, more like his old self again. As Fritzi retired, Sawyer and Melissa headed back to the main part of the house.

"Your jacket's in the kitchen. Let me run and get it for you. I don't have extra blankets, so you'll need it if it gets chilly." Melissa went one way and Sawyer walked into the living room, eyeing his choices.

Yes, there was a recliner, but it was built for a woman and looked secondhand and would surely break if Sawyer tried to lean back and stretch out on it. That left the sofa— which wasn't built to his dimensions—or the floor. He'd camped out under the stars before, with nothing more than a sleeping bag between him and the hard ground. "Sofa it is."

He pulled off the two upright cushions and piled them on the recliner, then unhooked his belt and removed his gun and holster. He tucked them under a pair of throw pillows at one end of the sofa and began unbuttoning the denim shirt he wore.

He was untucking the tails of his shirt when he heard Melissa's voice in the hall. "I went ahead and set the coffeemaker for tomorrow morning. I hope you don't mind that I tried on your jacket last night. I promise I didn't wrinkle it or—" She stopped in the archway, hugging his jacket to her chest and staring at his. "What are you doing?"

"Making myself comfortable. I've slept on couches before."

It seemed to require a considerable amount of effort to raise her gaze up to his. "But I thought…that when you said you were staying the night that you'd be…armed and dangerous—sitting up in the kitchen. Something like that." She was checking out the gap at the front of his shirt again.

Oh, man. It wasn't sympathy that was making her pupils dilate like that. His entire body seemed to dilate in response to her innocent desire. Hell. Did she even know she was lusting after him? And after that whole exchange in Benjamin's bedroom, when he'd wanted...so much...he was dying to give her anything she asked for.

Don't push it, Kincaid. If he intended to remain as professional and vigilant about moving in as he'd promised himself he'd be—if he intended to prove he was a better man than Longbow—he was going to have to button his shirt and make a joke. Or else she was going to have to blink.

Sawyer started with the bottom button of his shirt. "I haven't had much sleep lately, and I need to get *some* shut-eye if I'm going to stay sharp. Since there's no spare bedroom, it's either the couch or your front porch, and I figured even you had enough sympathy that you wouldn't make me sleep out in the rain."

"I wouldn't."

"Of course, there is a third option." Her blue eyes had locked onto his again, but he dutifully kept buttoning. "I know from fixing the windows last night that somebody has a double bed all to herself."

That shocked her out of gaping and

tempered her interest, though the beautiful blush on her cheeks was almost worth the un-gentlemanly innuendo. She tossed his jacket onto the couch and spun away. "I'll get you a pillow."

A half hour later, Sawyer was twisting on the couch, trying to decide whether he'd be more comfortable letting his feet dangle over the arm of the sofa, or sitting up straighter so he could get rid of the crick in his neck. Ha! What had he said about getting some shut-eye? He'd tried to tease Melissa out of that unconscious longing in her eyes so he could remember he was here for business, not pleasure.

But the joke was on him.

The pillow she'd brought him must have come straight from her bed. Her feminine, unperfumed scent was all around him—on his clothes now, on his skin—intensified by the darkness in the room, made more intimate by the soft patter of rain against the windows and porch roof.

Instead of relaxing for a couple of hours, he'd sentenced himself to an ironic test of fortitude. He'd either have to stay awake, or find a way to monitor his sleep to keep from having erotic dreams about Melissa.

Slowly undressing in the darkness. Shyly offering herself to him. Trusting him. Wanting him. Inviting him to touch. Learning every delicate curve of her body by scent or stroke or taste alone. Tapping into bottled-up emotions and frustrated desires. Boldly…

"Ah, hell."

Sawyer tossed the pillow and swung his feet to the floor. He raked all ten fingers through his hair and rubbed at the stubble on his jaw, trying to shake the images that heated his body and left him ready to bust out of his skin. Who needed erotic dreams when he could torture his self-control perfectly well while he was wide awake?

He needed to cool off. Though he'd conceded to propriety by leaving his shirt on, he quickly unbuttoned it again as he rose to his feet and stalked across the room to the front windows. Nudging aside the curtain and shade, he peered through the window, surveying the night outside.

The rain was keeping things quiet, but it also limited his vision. He could barely make out the gray sedan across the street, and the surveillance van two houses down was completely invisible. That itch under his skin transformed into something wary and crept up the back of his neck.

There was more than Ace Longbow or Holt's lousy plan to worry about here. The torrent running down the middle of the street came up to the hubcaps on the feds' sedan. He wondered if it was worth a call to find out if the street's runoff fed into a detention cell or one of the creeks and rivers in the area, and whether the sewer system was able to handle all this. Another inch and the water would be up over the curb and flooding the yard. Melissa's little Pontiac would be useless plowing through deep water. And flooded streets would make it difficult for emergency vehicles—and backup—to get to the house quickly.

The chill radiating through the glass might be cooling his body, but a different kind of alertness was fueling his adrenaline now. Trusting nothing to Riley Holt or Mother Nature, Sawyer went back to the sofa to pull out his gun and tuck it into the back of his jeans beneath his shirt. Even with all the cameras and watchful eyes out there, a man on foot, dressed in black, could sneak right up to the house without being detected.

Moving silently through the shadowy

house, Sawyer wedged a kitchen chair beneath the front doorknob to reinforce the locks. Then he did a systematic check of all the windows, just as he had before turning in.

Even though the opening would be too small for a full-grown man to climb through, he was in the bathroom, securing the window in the shower, when his cell phone vibrated in his pocket.

He checked the number. Unfamiliar, but it had a KCPD prefix. He answered by the third ring. "Kincaid."

The woman's voice sounded unusually loud in the hushed quiet of the house. "This is Dr. Masterson. Holly—from the crime lab. I'm not calling too late, am I? I'm sorry, but I keep late hours—I usually work the night shift at the lab."

"Trust me, I'm awake." Sawyer moved the conversation back into the living room so that he wouldn't wake the sleeping family.

"I wanted to call with the preliminary autopsy report on James McBride's murder." Talk about efficiency. Sawyer checked his watch. If was after midnight. "Is this a good time?"

"As good as any. But J. R. Hendricks has the lead on the case. You should try him first."

"I did. I left a message on his voice mail. I wanted to apologize for my behavior this morning, too. Sometimes I get too focused on my work, but that's no excuse to be rude." He heard some clicking in the background, and then, "Oh, damn. Not another one. What the hell is going on here?"

"Dr. Masterson?" If this woman was as big a flake as she sounded, then he had more important things to deal with tonight. "Is everything all right?"

"I'm sorry. Somebody's gotten into my archived computer files and deleted information. Or there's a glitch in the system or…I don't know. But I don't forget things. I know that information was here."

Swiping a hand across his jaw, Sawyer schooled his patience. "Maybe this isn't the best time for you. You should call J.R. in the morning."

"No. Wait. I'll deal with that later. I think I've found something that may be important." Her tone had changed. Whatever fits her computer was giving her, she sounded lucid and calm—and as detached from her emotions as he'd expect a medical examiner to be. "James McBride used to be a much bigger man. I'd have to take a look at his medical records to see if the size discrepancy is related to his heart condition, but I'd say he's lost eighty to a hundred pounds in the past year."

Sawyer blew a tight breath between his lips. He definitely had more important things to worry about tonight. "Listen, Doc—I'm concentrating on those two surviving fugitives who escaped from Jeff City. You can e-mail the autopsy report to my computer at work, and I'll read it when I get in next week."

"I'm sorry, I'm not saying this right. You know, I work with dead bodies and a very small staff or on my own, so conversation isn't always my best—"

"Doc!" In his brain, he yelled. Out loud he kept his voice to a whisper. "E-mail me the information."

He pulled the phone away to hang up.

"It's about your father!"

Sawyer put the phone back to his ear. "I thought this was about James McBride."

"It is."

"Forget about making conversation. Just make sense and tell me the facts."

She sounded as relieved as he was to be moving on. "Mr. McBride had a tattoo. I wouldn't have noticed it except for the weight loss that left his skin stretched out. Otherwise, the tattoo would have been very small, almost undetectable and could be mistaken for a birthmark."

"And you're telling me this because…?"

"I've seen that mark before. On other cases." She was typing on her computer again. "I can't seem to find any of that information right now, but I know I've seen that tattoo before."

"How does this relate to my father?"

"He had a mark like that. Like a tiny, almost microscopic number three."

It was the second conversation in a day that indicated the two murders could be related. "Send it to my brother Atticus as soon as you can." He was the one who could read and make sense of reports. Better than Sawyer could when he was so preoccupied with Melissa's troubles, at any rate. "And, Doc? Thank you."

Chapter Eight

"Sawyer?"

Melissa saw his broad shoulders tense, and hugged her arms tighter around her waist. He hadn't heard her tiptoeing through the hallway. Just what kind of trouble was he expecting, talking on the phone so late at night and wearing his gun to sleep in?

The holster outlined at the waist of his jeans worried her more than it reassured her. "I heard you on the phone out here. Has something happened? Did Ace call? Or Agent Holt?"

Long sleeves and cotton pajama pants couldn't stop the wave of goose bumps that washed over her. She'd chilled inside and out, hearing his whispered, urgent, commanding voice. Something was wrong.

A controlling breath eased the tension from his back as he pocketed his phone and turned. With only a few night-lights on in the house to give them illumination, it was hard to make out his facial expression. She needed to hear his voice. "Talk to me, Sawyer. Keeping me in the dark about Ace doesn't make me feel safe."

"Hey." He moved a step closer. She tensed. Dreaded. And then a gentle touch through the shadows brushed across her cheek, defusing her fears. Melissa unwound her arms and wrapped them around Sawyer's waist as he gathered her in. She burrowed against him, pressing her cheek to bare skin and musky heat, warming herself against the steady beat of his heart. With one hand anchored possessively at her hip, the other tangled in her hair, massaging her nape. "I'm not keeping anything from you, sweetheart. I didn't mean to spook you. That was work. Another investigation. Possibly a new lead on Dad's case. The call had nothing to do with Ace."

"Are you sure?" Her fingers touched the unforgiving steel of his gun and she shivered. "Don't lie, thinking you're protecting me." She fumbled to find supple skin and human warmth, and ended up clutching two fistfuls of soft cotton. "If I'd understood all the lies back in the beginning, when I first thought I loved him, I never would have made such a horrible mess of everything. I wouldn't be stuck in this shell of a life—trapped in my own home, always looking over my shoulder. I wouldn't have sentenced my mother and son—and now you—to this nightmare."

"None of this is your fault, Mel. Back then…" His hands moved to cup her jaw and lift her face to meet his downturned expression. His eyes were dark as molasses in the shadows, but clear in their intent as his mouth descended toward hers. "…or now."

Sawyer's mouth opened, hot and moist and gentle, over hers. He stroked his tongue between her lips, lapping at the softer skin inside. If he was testing her resistance, he'd find none. Not on this lonely dark chill of a night. Melissa curled her fingers into the front of his shirt and held on, shyly sliding her tongue against his. The texture was raspy and ticklish, like a cat's—yet there was more mountain lion than tabby in the coiled strength beneath the palm of her hands.

Then, with a guttural moan, low in his throat, the kiss changed. Sawyer's mouth grew hard, demanding. For a fraction of an instant, it blotted out her fears, her doubts, her protests. In one heartbeat, she was too stunned to respond. In the next, she was pushing onto her toes and clinging to his neck and yielding to his rightful claim. He was raw and male, and Melissa caught fire deep inside, giving birth to an all-powerful goddess who tasted passion, took comfort and demanded as much as she was given. Freely.

Melissa didn't know if she was laughing or crying. Emotions trapped too close to the surface for too long erupted into a fever of need that had her nearly climbing up Sawyer's body to find that perfect fit of mouths, curves and planes, and desires. His hair was chocolate silk between her fingers, his shoulders a sheltering mountain. His hands roamed up and down her back, sliding beneath her shirt to brand her cool skin, then reaching down to squeeze her bottom and lift her off the floor.

The tips of her breasts beaded into nubby pearls as she fell into his chest, sending fiery ribbons of need straight to her womb. She wrapped her legs around his waist and held on as he carried her across the room and sat on the couch, turning her sideways across his lap. "This is crazy," she whispered against his mouth, abrading her swollen lips on the raspy stubble of his beard and loving the sharp contrast of male and female. She drew her hands beneath the collar of his shirt, skimming her palms over hot flesh and smooth swells of muscle that quivered and danced beneath her curious exploration. "I shouldn't want something this badly."

"Or need someone this much." His hands wandered at will beneath her knit top, while his lips cruised over her jaw and discovered a particularly sensitive spot along the column of her neck. Melissa threw her head back, panting as the tickle became a seduction and the seduction became a willing surrender.

"Is this what it's supposed to be like? I can't—" She gasped as his big palm closed over her naked breast, soothing and arousing her all at once. "I can't think."

"Don't think." He veed his legs and Melissa sank between them, feeling the unmistakable bulge of his desire pressing against her bottom. Her hands stilled their foray beneath his shirt as the first twinge of a bad memory pierced the haze of instinctive passion. "Just feel."

She kissed his chin. The strong line of his jaw.

But Sawyer was moving beneath her. One big hand had locked onto her hip, trapping him against his arousal. His touch grew stronger, his kisses more needy. A wall went up inside Melissa's head. Old memories. *Different man.* Old hurts. *Not this man.* Ace. *Sawyer.*

But the rational arguments couldn't make the uncertainty recede. Melissa pushed against his chest and scooted up onto Sawyer's thigh, forcing some cool air between them. "We're exhausted," she tried to reason. Her fingers stopped clutching, though she couldn't seem to pull them away. "We've been dealing with so much, maybe we're just reacting. This may not be what either of us wants."

"It's what I want." He kissed the hollow of her throat. Kissed her collarbone. "*You're* what I want." He raised his head and looked her in the eye, his breathing coming in deep, ragged gasps that matched the rise and fall of her own chest. "*I'm* not what you want?"

She stroked the firm line of his collarbone through his shirt. Sampling the irresistible? Or apologizing? "I think you might be."

"You think?" His head fell back and he blew a deep sigh into the air before looking at her again. "You're hard on a man's ego, woman."

Definitely apologizing. She curled her fingers into her palm. "I don't mean to be. I told you I was pretty screwed up. It doesn't make any sense to want someone but not *want*…everything."

"Moving too fast for you, huh?"

"Maybe. I'm not sure."

He leaned back into the couch, reaching behind him to remove his gun and set it on the cushion beside him before settling in a straight-backed position. He rubbed his other hand up and down her arm, as though reluctant to completely break the physical contact between them. "If you're not sure…do you want to stop?"

"I want…to slow down." Her gaze fell to the zipper of his jeans. He, clearly, was ready to go all the way. Hastily, she tugged his shirt together at the collar and smoothed her palms across the wrinkles she'd made there. "I know that's unfair to you. I didn't mean to give you the wrong idea." Maybe she should just cut and run and go back to the relative security of her room. "I'm sorry."

"That son of a bitch." Melissa froze mid-scramble. Sawyer framed her face in his hands. His eyes searched her face, no doubt reading her fear. And then everything in him relaxed. "I'm sorry. That was for your ex. He didn't take no for an answer, did he."

She hated talking about this. Only her counselor and attorney and a sealed court record knew. "Sometimes. When it was that time of the month. I learned to lie and say it was."

"Give me a minute, okay?" When he let her go, Melissa crawled over to the corner of the sofa and curled her legs up to her chest, hugging herself for warmth as she watched the rage darken his expression. He dug his fingers into his thighs so hard, she thought he might rip through the denim.

But then his grip relaxed, his skin lightened to its healthy tan shade and his mouth softened into a less formidable line.

"You scared of me?" he asked, his voice barely a whisper in the shadows.

Was she? He certainly was an emotional man—felt things deeply, spoke his mind, possessed a working vocabulary of curse words. But he hadn't hurt her. Hadn't hurt her son or mother. And now, when the only other man she'd known would have been forcing himself on her or making it clear how much she'd disappointed him, Sawyer was sitting quietly at the opposite end of the sofa—talking.

Something brittle and cold crumbled inside Melissa, leaving an unfamiliar warmth and newfound hope in its place. She released the grip on her legs and changed her posture to a more open position.

"No. I'm not afraid of you."

"Good." His mouth curved into a wry smile. "You shouldn't be afraid of sex and gettin' turned on, either. Or making me all hot and bothered."

He held out his hand, an offering, a request. Melissa took it. She took his hand and he tugged her back across the couch to sit beside him. "You're supposed to tell the man you're with what you want or don't want. He's supposed to listen. There aren't consequences for being honest. If this is moving too fast, you're right to say so."

"But—"

"No buts. Not with me."

That wall of fear and doubt disintegrated further. The spirit of the teenage girl she'd once been—that hopeful innocent who once believed in nice guys and happy endings—was still inside her, after all. Melissa threw her arms around Sawyer's neck and hugged him tight before pulling away and curling her legs beneath her on the cushion beside him. "Is it okay if we just cuddle for a bit?"

That sounded like a goofy request from a grown woman. But he seemed pleased that she'd asked. Sawyer Kincaid was a handsome man when he smiled. He draped his arm behind her back and tucked her to his side. "We can cuddle all night long if that's what you want."

She turned her cheek into the pillow of his shoulder. "I knew when you walked into that bar last year that you were a nice guy."

"Yeah, but let's not let that rumor get out."

"Your secret's safe with me, tough guy."

The phone rang on the kitchen wall and that young woman's spirit died once more. The passion was gone, the teasing over, the mood broken.

Melissa forced herself to breathe and climbed to her feet. Sawyer stood beside her. "You don't have to answer."

Another ominous ring beckoned her from the shadows. "I do if I'm not going to let him rule my life anymore."

"Then we'll do it together." He took her hand and led her into the kitchen, turning on the lights along the way.

"It's the same number as before," she read. "Ace."

Sawyer pulled out his cell phone and punched in a number. "Answer it. I'm right here." He took her hand before turning away to make a call of his own. "It's him. Are you getting this?"

While Sawyer alerted the surveillance team, she picked up the receiver. "Hello?"

"I saw you this morning, little one." How she hated that belittling endearment. "Other than that mark on your face, you're as beautiful as ever."

She squeezed Sawyer's hand, needing strength.

"You're doing fine, sweetheart," he whispered. "Keep him talking as long as you can. They're starting the trace."

"What do you want, Ace?"

"To hear your voice. I always liked the soft sound of it. Thought it was sexy. Listening to your voice has always had a way of soothing my temper."

So what were the slaps in the face or twisted wrists about? Why had he dragged her down to the river and thrown her against a rock wall if a conversation like she'd just shared with Sawyer would do?

She wrung the life out of Sawyer's hand, but he didn't question her need, didn't complain. He just held on.

"Thanks, I guess. Where are you?"

He laughed. "Now, you know I'm not gonna tell you that. You've got cops listening in. They were swarming all over you at the diner today."

She glanced up at Sawyer. "He knows."

He signaled her to keep Ace on the line.

Nodding, Melissa swallowed her revulsion and kept on talking. "You always were smarter than me. I never could fool you on anything."

"I'm smarter than all those cops, too. I've been a free man for almost three days now. I walked right under their noses yesterday. They've got nothin' on me." He paused.

"Ace?"

"Hold on a second, little one."

She heard running footsteps echoing in the background, and then a crash. "What the hell are you doin', man?"

Melissa frowned. "Is someone with you?"

"Mayweather?" Sawyer mouthed the question.

She heard a grunt. Another crash. Ace was panting hard into the phone now.

"What's going on?" she asked.

"Taking care of some business."

There was a curse, and then she heard a man screaming at Ace. "You want a piece of me, chief? You come get me! I took care of that old man. I can take care of you, too. And I'll do that job for free."

"You should have run farther and faster, Tyrell."

A trio of gunshots exploded in Melissa's ear, startling the breath from her. "Ace?"

Sawyer was instantly beside her, his hand steadying her shaky grip. He'd heard them, too.

"Ace!"

Heavy, labored breathing finally answered her. "I have to go now, little one. I may not be able to see you for a while. But I'll come back for you when the coast is clear. We'll be together again. Just you and me. I promise." Ace's low voice lightened with arrogance. "I know the cops are listening in on this line, trying to trace this call. I know just how long they need to find me. So I'm hanging up now. I love you."

The click in her ear was as deafening as the gunfire had been.

Melissa's fingers were numb when Sawyer

finally pried the receiver from her hand and turned her cold body into the warmth of his chest.

"EXCELLENT JOB, Mr. Longbow." The boss stepped over Tyrell Mayweather's body, carefully avoiding the blood still pooling on the warehouse's concrete floor. The boss pointed to a slug in the wall from Tyrell's missed shot. "Make sure we remove this evidence, and take Mr. Mayweather's gun to dispose of."

Meanwhile, Ace replaced the spent cartridges in the magazine and reloaded his gun. It was an old habit, one he'd learned back in South Dakota when he'd taken his first enforcement job, working for a loan shark. Keep your gun loaded. Keep your eyes on your enemy. Never surrender your advantage. Because the man with the strongest hand wins.

It was a lesson this boss knew, too. The suit was different, but equally expensive, meant to show off wealth, to intimidate. The albino with the tats followed a few steps behind, playing cleanup crew or bodyguard or whatever was required of him, Ace suspected. The white-haired man had spent some time behind bars, too, according to the designs on his pale skin.

But Ace had an advantage of his own. Knowledge. "I see how things are. You got us out of prison to do your dirty work. Hank messed with KCPD's computers, losing evidence on crimes I imagine you had a lot to do with. Tyrell took out that old man and made it look like a gang hit to throw off any personal connection you might have to him. And then I eliminate both those stupid bastards so no one can trace either job back to you. I imagine with our different talents, different styles, it'd be impossible for the cops to put together any kind of pattern to even link the crimes."

"I thought you'd be the cleverest of the three. I'm pleased to see you haven't disappointed me." That chase through the warehouse may have taken a bigger toll on Ace than he'd first realized. He was still breathing just as hard as he'd been when he'd cornered Tyrell and fired the kill shot. He gave himself permission to sit on the edge of a crate to rest, but he kept the gun in his hand, resting on his thigh, in case he needed to use it again. "How's the shoulder?"

"I'm still alive, aren't I?" He'd considered

infection and how he might get his hands on some antibiotics. But since he hadn't bled to death yet, Ace doubted that would be the cause. "I don't know how long that's gonna last, though. I thought I was gettin' out of prison to get away from a hit. But I'm next on your list now, aren't I." He nodded toward the albino. "Is he here to eliminate me?"

"No."

Ace laughed. Melissa had been right when she said he was smart. The boss could see that, too. "You mean not yet. You haven't killed me yet, so you must have another job for me, right?"

"I keep my word. As I said, you've fulfilled your responsibility. I consider the cost of your freedom a debt paid in full. Now get out of the country. Live a long life without ever thinking of me again."

"There's no trick to this?"

"No trick."

Ace stood, disappointed that there wouldn't be more money or work coming his way, but thinking it was best to leave while he still could.

"Oh, did I tell you? I saw your wife."

Ex-wife. The correction formed on the tip of Ace's tongue—an internal voice that tried to get past the delusions and denials and warn him of something. He was being played. But Ace couldn't seem to help himself. He had to ask. "How do you know Melissa?"

"So pretty. Feminine and delicate. A natural blonde if I'm not mistaken."

"Where did you see my wife?" Too late, the inner voice tried to warn. He'd just lost his advantage.

"She was with another man. Big guy like you. A cop, I think. Yes, I'm sure he was wearing a gun."

"Cops have been watching her 24/7 since my escape. They're all around her. I've seen her, too. Could have touched her if I'd wanted."

"This cop touched her. He wasn't there professionally, I don't think. He had his hands all over her. Kissed her." The boss turned to leave. But just before the albino opened the door to the street, the boss came back. "I hear he's staying the night at her house. Shacking up with her. He was probably lying in bed beside her while you were chatting with her on the phone just now."

The rage swelled up inside, nearly blinding him. Instead of thinking about how the boss could have known he was talking to Melissa, all he could think of was her spreading her legs for some other man. How could she cheat on him when he'd been faithful to her? How could she lie with someone else when she was all he'd ever wanted?

"Leave the country, Mr. Longbow."

"Not without my wife."

Chapter Nine

Melissa was beginning to think the sun was never going to shine again. Literally or figuratively.

"Two down and one to go. Thank God." Pearl Jenkins tutted at the television screen hanging in the corner of the diner. She hugged her arm around Melissa, standing at the counter beside her. "It must be a good feeling to know that the authorities are closing in on your ex-husband. All this craziness will be over soon enough."

Or maybe the craziness would never end. How did Ace continue to stay one step ahead of trained federal agents? And why couldn't he give up on the idea of *them*? She'd divorced him after three years of marriage. But it had taken two years after that—when he was finally sentenced to prison—to get him out of her life. If Ace was never captured, the terror would never stop.

There would always be a phone call in the middle of the night. There would always be an unread letter, promising vile things. There would always be the flash of movement out of the corner of her eye that would make her think he was there. Watching. Waiting.

She could never move forward with her life. Never live without wondering what lurked in the shadows. Never love.

Sawyer's whiskey-colored eyes watched her across the counter, over the rim of his coffee cup. He knew what she was thinking, fearing.

And bless his heart, he thought he could make it all right for her and her family if he cared enough. Was patient enough. Smart enough. He thought her life could be fixed, and that eventually they could move on—together.

What nice guys like Sawyer Kincaid didn't understand was that her life was like a broken toy with a part missing. You could put it back together, but it would never work right. It would never be normal or whole again.

Melissa jumped as Pearl clapped her hands and shooed the cooks back into the kitchen, and the waitresses onto the floor. "Okay, boys and girls, show's over. We've got cus-tomers waiting to eat. Let's move."

"You okay?" Sawyer asked.

"I just need to keep moving," Melissa decided. She set a stack of napkins beside the silverware bin and started rolling a paper square around each place setting. "Quit thinking and worrying for a while."

Yeah, like that was going to happen.

"Give that wounded part a chance to heal?"

She nodded and got busy, surprised yet pleased that he'd remembered her words.

Pearl turned down the volume of Hayley Resnick's morning news report about the black man shot to death at a CT Labs storage facility in the K.C. suburb of Lenexa, Kansas. Then she scuttled off into the kitchen to whip up another batch of blueberry muffins.

But instead of being distracted by her work and getting some relief from the pall over her life that was Ace's legacy, Melissa grew more discouraged and more unsure with every passing minute. The words scrolled across the bottom of the television screen as the station went back to a live feed at the ware-house. *Authorities have positively identified the slain man as Tyrell Mayweather, the second of three prison escapees to turn up dead in the Kansas City area. The third escapee, Richard Longbow, is still at large.*

An image of Ace filled the screen—dramatic high cheekbones; black, shoulder-length hair that reminded her so much of Benjamin; cold black eyes that reminded her of nothing but conscienceless terror. *Authorities at this time consider Longbow a person of interest in both Mayweather's and Henry Drennerman's shooting deaths. However, according to Federal Agent Riley Holt, who masterminded the search for the three fugitives, they are now considering the possibility that Longbow might also have shared a tragic fate similar to his fellow prisoners. If you have any information...*

"Mastermind, my ass. Holt's botched this recovery operation from the very beginning." Sawyer's wry opinion of Riley Holt diverted Melissa's attention from the TV, but couldn't make the horrific memory that was still so fresh in her mind fade.

"We heard that murder on the phone last night. I know Ace pulled that trigger—at the same time he was saying he loved me and wanted to be with me...he was killing a man."

Sawyer reached across the counter and folded Melissa's ice-cold hand in his. "You said you heard three shots. There were only two bullets in Mayweather. Chances are Longbow took that third bullet. Holt said his men found traces of blood that match Ace's type."

Melissa nodded, trying to find hope in Sawyer's words but coming up short. "His men combed that warehouse from top to bottom. They didn't find anyone but Mayweather. Ace is still alive. I feel it in my bones. He's still out there, closer than anybody thinks."

The bell over the door rang and Riley Holt held open the door for a pair of customers. He crossed to the table where two of his men were sitting, eating their breakfast. They exchanged words in hushed voices, and all three of them glanced her way at least once during the conversation.

"That's reassuring." Trepidation seemed to bring out the sarcasm in her.

Sawyer glanced over his shoulder, silently fuming on her behalf when he turned back to face her. "Don't let them get to you. Like I said, recapturing Longbow is their priority, not you or your feelings." His handsome mouth curved into a smile, making an attempt to cheer her again. "That's why I'm here. With Fritzi and Ben spending the day at Mom's house—with Holden and Atticus and their own contingent of agents watching over them—you've got me all to yourself. I've got nothing to do but watch you all day long."

"Lucky me." Melissa summoned half a smile for his sake, but she wasn't really feeling it. "If Ace was wounded in the escape, or again last night, then why hasn't he shown up at the morgue or at an emergency room somewhere?"

"I'd like an answer to that question myself." Riley Holt adjusted his tie as he came over and slid onto a stool beside Sawyer. "Coffee, please, ma'am?"

Melissa retrieved a clean mug and the coffeepot.

Three days of hunting down bad guys on next to no sleep was starting to show. The suit might be fresh, but the lines beside Agent Holt's eyes were grooved a little more deeply, and a weary cynicism colored his tone. "I still contend your ex has a friend on the outside, helping him. A connection we haven't been able to make—" he raised his mug in a mock toast to Melissa when she handed it to him "—or prove yet."

Sawyer pushed his own mug away and stood. "You're out of line, Holt."

"And you're too quick to defend her." He smiled, but there was no laughter in his voice. "You're not thinking like a cop on this, Kincaid. Where was she two days ago—the day Longbow escaped?" He gestured to Melissa as though she was nothing more than a visual aid—not a living, breathing innocent he was accusing of aiding and abetting a wanted felon. "She left work after the lunch hour, attended her evening accounting class. But no one can verify her whereabouts for the time in between."

"I was at the library, studying."

"For five hours?"

"It's the only afternoon I have off when my mom isn't working and she can stay with Benjamin. I had to research a paper and—"

"Don't say another word, Mel. He's baiting you. You've done nothing wrong."

"How many times do you think she spoke to Longbow before reporting that first phone call?"

"I didn't—"

"Maybe they were planning his escape together all along."

"Ace tried to kill me! Why would I help him?"

Holt took his time answering, savoring a

long, aromatic drink. "Trust me, Miss Teague, in my line of work? I've seen stranger relationships than yours and Longbow's."

"You're grabbing at straws, Holt. You mucked up this investigation and you know it." Sawyer's sweeping gaze took in the two agents behind Holt, the ceiling—indicating the sniper positioned above them—and on out through the diner's front window where even Melissa could see the agent patrolling the roof of the construction project across the street. "Your profiling and protocols didn't get the job done this time. The trail's run cold, and you're left with two dead bodies and a missing killer on the loose. Without any viable leads, you've got nothing to do but shadow Mel and hope like hell Longbow comes looking for her."

"Oh, he'll come." Holt sounded as certain as Melissa that she and Ace would cross paths soon. "And I'll be ready for him when he does."

"It's a crapshoot and you know it. Innocent people are gonna get hurt. That'll be on your head, too." The brown-eyed gaze softened as it slid over to Melissa. "If I thought she'd say yes, I'd pack up Mel and her family and take them away to some secluded, unnamed island not even on a map, where none of this could touch her."

She reached across the counter, feeling a sense of sadness as she touched Sawyer's wrist. "If I believed there really was a place like that, I'd say yes."

He turned his hand to take hold of hers. "Let me show you—"

A high whistling sound pierced the morning outside, stopping conversation and condemnations, and turning everyone's attention to the window. It sounded just like the Fourth of July, a fiery celebration screaming through the air.

Only this was April.

"What the hell?"

Sawyer looked at Holt. Holt looked at Sawyer.

And then there was a beat of silence.

"Son of a bitch."

Sawyer leaped up over the counter, slinging his arms around Melissa as he dived for the floor. "Get down!"

They hit the rubber mat hard as the world on the other side of the counter exploded into a million pieces.

Tucking her head into his shoulder, Sawyer rolled Melissa beneath him as a millisecond later the front window shattered and shards of flying glass rained down around them like hailstones.

Melissa could barely breathe beneath the crushing weight of Sawyer's body. But she held on tight to his jacket at his biceps, feeling the pummel of falling debris through every flinch of his muscle. "My God," she breathed against the worn leather at her cheek. "What's happening?"

"Explosion in the construction site across the street."

Riley Holt shouted from the other side of the counter. "It's like the damn courthouse in Jeff City. An artillery shell. Where the hell is he gettin' this stuff?"

"Everybody okay?" Sawyer shouted once the downpour had stopped and the chatter of shocked voices began. There were a few yeses from around the diner, and groans of pain that worried Melissa more than the detailed reports of cuts and bruises. He pushed up on his elbows, brushing her hair off her face. "What about you? One piece?"

She nodded. She plucked slivers of glass from his hair and collar. "Are you hurt?"

He dropped his head, capturing her mouth

in a swift, potent kiss, then pulling away just as quickly. "One piece."

A waterfall of glass fell from his jacket as he rolled off her and pulled her to a sitting position.

"Stay down until we know it's clear." Sawyer squeezed her shoulder before scooting to the end of the counter and surveying the damage.

"Stay down?" Melissa had already pulled her legs beneath her and matched his squatting position. "There are people hurt. I have to help."

"You have to stay put." He pulled out his phone and dialed 911.

"There's a first-aid kit right here." She grabbed the plastic box from behind the counter and duckwalked out behind him, balancing her hand against his shoulder to peek out with him.

She'd seen pictures of war zones before. But she'd never been in the middle of one. "Oh, Sawyer. What…?"

But she had a sick feeling she knew why this had happened.

What wasn't broken had been knocked over. What wasn't nailed down had been thrown toward the diner's back wall. Rain blew in through the open space that had once been Pearl's prize window, along with the smell of smoke. An entire brick wall had collapsed on the warehouse being remodeled across the street. Men in hard hats appeared from a rising cloud of dust through an archway onto the sidewalk, cursing and coughing, then running and pointing up as a second wall began to crumble and topple over above their heads.

As Sawyer cautiously pushed to his feet, she saw Riley Holt shake the debris from his coat, rising from his knees to his feet to meet Sawyer halfway.

"Are you thinking what I'm thinking?" Holt pulled out a white handkerchief and tied it around the cut on his hand.

"I hate to say it, but yeah…"

The two men who had been rivals spoke as one.

"Diversion."

With a nod that must have communicated something that only law men would understand, both men snapped into action. Sawyer offered Melissa a hand to stand, but wouldn't let her budge from behind the relative safety of the diner's counter. He turned his attention to the phone. "We've had an explosion up on

Fifth Street in the City Market District. We need multiple buses," he ordered, referring to ambulances and paramedics, "fire and traffic control ASAP."

Holt pointed to his agents as he ran for the door. "You, stay with Miss Teague and tend to the wounded here. The rest of you are with me. I want this block locked down. I want every vehicle stopped and searched, even the ones with the flashing lights." He motioned back to Sawyer. "Can you secure this building?"

"I'm not leaving her."

"I guess I figured as much. I'll handle it. Will you at least take charge of the scene here?"

Sawyer nodded. "Will do."

Before Sawyer ever turned, Melissa gave him a nudge forward. "I know. Stay put. Don't worry, I'm not going anywhere." She gestured to the sea of glass and debris around her. "There's plenty I can do to help right here."

He planted his feet and turned, anyway. "I'm just going to do a quick 360 around the building, make sure the other entrances are intact."

Melissa reached up and brushed another flake of glass from his collar. "Go. I don't want this on my conscience. Make sure everyone's okay."

He grabbed her hand and planted a kiss in her palm. "Stay. Put."

Sawyer Kincaid in action was a thing to behold. Despite his size, he moved with a graceful precision and sense of purpose that inspired confidence and spurred Melissa into action. Crunching the glass beneath her feet, she hurried over to the woman holding a bloodied napkin to the wound on her forehead.

Ten minutes later, the battle zone had been organized into structured chaos. If she was a little antsy about Sawyer taking longer than she'd expected, Melissa didn't have time to worry. Customers and employees from this and other businesses along the block who weren't injured were out front, helping paramedics move patients, sweeping up broken glass or fortifying brick walls to prevent further injuries. Firefighters had the blaze under control and were inspecting the surrounding buildings for unseen structural damage and secondary fires.

Melissa had graduated to assistant EMT, holding equipment and holding hands to help calm patients. After one of Holt's agents brought in a group of traumatized construction workers to be checked out, the EMT sent her back to the kitchen. "Go soak some clean towels in water. Some of these men who aren't hurt badly will still want to clean up and cool off."

"Sure."

Backing through the swinging metal door, Melissa untied her bloodstained apron and threw it into the trash as she hurried by. "Steve? It's just me." She called to the cook who the fire department had sent inside to make sure the gas ovens had been turned off. She picked up the flashlight sitting on the plating counter. "I'm going to borrow your light, okay?" But there was no answer. "Steve?"

Hmm. She must have missed him when he came back out. As busy as everyone had been, the fire chief could have easily put him on another detail and she wouldn't have known it. Still, being alone made her a little antsy, so she turned on the light and got started.

With the ovens off and the food inside forgotten, the dishwasher had shut down with a tray of plates halfway through the cycle when the fire department had cut the power to the block. Melissa went about her work, pretending the eerily silent kitchen didn't make her think of ghost towns or science-fiction stories where an evil alien makes everyone disappear in the middle of whatever they were doing.

She kept moving. Kept working. Kept making noise. She stopped up the sinks and turned on the faucets, then scrounged through shelves and drawers, finding large pans and clean towels.

But when she turned off the water and wrung out the first towel, something scuttled past the back-door exit into the alley. Melissa tensed. Then relief rippled from head to toe once she identified the sound. She fished the second towel from the sink. Oh man, if the mice had been chased inside by all the rain, Pearl was going to have a fit. Hell, *she* was going to have a fit if she ran across one of them while she was back here.

She plopped the second towel on a tray and reached for the third.

Her mouse breathed.

"Steve? Is that you? Pearl? I thought the paramedics sent you home to rest." Silence. "Sawyer?"

He could have come in through the back door. Only, the back door was closed.

She picked up the heavy metal flashlight again, turning it in her hand like a club.

Move.

The instinct to run propelled her toward the swinging door before the danger even registered in her brain. She needed to get back to people. Back to a well-lit room.

Back to Sawyer.

The hands grabbed her from behind. Covered her scream and lifted her high off the floor.

She whacked at the shoulder behind her, but it was a glancing blow, earning a curse and a slam up against the counter where his body pinned her and he wrenched the flashlight from her hand. For one awful instant she thought the light was going to come smashing down on her skull, but her attacker reconsidered. He tossed the light into the water and jerked her back up against him. Cruel fingers dug into her jaw and waist as he picked her up.

His hot breath crept over her cheek. His cheek felt clammy against hers. His grip was hard, his bonds unbreakable as he carried her, kicking and writhing and screaming in muffled futility, toward the alley exit.

He paused only long enough to kick open the door and rasp against her ear, "Shh, little one. Told you I'd come back for you. Now be still. I don't want to have to hurt you."

"WHERE'S MELISSA?"

Sawyer had a bad feeling about this.

The first of Holt's men sent him over to where the second was helping Pearl Jenkins into a wheelchair.

"Pearl, have you seen Melissa?"

Pearl glanced around, frowning. "She was here a minute ago. My goodness. I just can't believe…"

Kind as the woman had been to Mel, when she started going on about her palpitations and being ready to retire, he moved on to the next patient. And the next.

Sure, they'd all seen Mel. *Past tense.* She'd been so helpful, so calming and gentle with them.

"Mel!" Sawyer's holler bounced off the empty walls.

His quick mission had taken a few minutes too long. He'd climbed onto the roof and found an access door to an adjoining building standing wide open. It had probably been forced open by the blast, but it provided an easy way to get inside the diner without being seen. So he'd pulled his gun and hauled his ass back downstairs.

Now he was here and Mel was gone.

But she'd promised she'd stay put.

"Try the kitchen." The busy EMT barely looked up from the arm he was bandaging.

And Sawyer didn't wait to thank him.

"Mel?" The metal door squealed on its hinges as Sawyer shoved his way in.

Too dark in here. Too many places to hide. Too damn quiet.

Pulling out his flashlight, he quickly spotted the towels on the tray, and a flashlight floating in the sink. He swung the light around until it landed on the white towel lying in a heap on the floor by the back door.

"Oh, no. No. No!"

Icy talons squeezed Sawyer's heart when he picked up the soggy towel and inspected it more closely. Three dark red spots marbled its bleached sterility.

Blood.

Sawyer swore.

He tore open the door and jumped down into the alley, whipping back and forth. He searched from side to side, from brick to brick. All he found was a pile of garbage bags and the unconscious cook beside the trash bin.

The rain beat down like millions of tiny fists, damning him for being too late. "Mel!"

He spun around. Again. And again.

Damn, he hated the rain.

It washed away footprints, drowned out the sounds of a struggle or scream. And it had swallowed up the woman he loved.

Chapter Ten

"Damn it, Holt—I'm not trusting you anymore." Sawyer tossed his jacket into the cab of Holden's truck and strapped on the extra flak vest from his SWAT gear.

In forty-five minutes, he'd assembled two brothers, a handful of friends, like J. R. Hendricks and Seth Cartwright, a respectable arsenal, and he'd memorized every cross street and doorway off this alley behind Pearl's Diner for a six-block stretch in either direction.

It had taken Riley Holt twice that long to realize his last fugitive had slipped through his fingers.

"You're the one who said he was going to stay with her. Where did *you* disappear to?" Holt retorted.

Sawyer palmed the center of Holt's chest and shoved him up against the alley's brick wall. "Don't you think I'm already beatin' myself up over that?"

"Easy, big guy." Atticus lay a cautionary hand on Sawyer's arm. "You won't do her any good if you get yourself arrested."

Sawyer bore down on Holt's unblinking eyes, looking for some flicker of remorse, some admission of guilt, some indication that he was feeling even one iota of the pain that was tearing him from the inside out.

And then the blue eyes blinked. "I screwed up, okay? Is that what you want to hear?"

"You thought Melissa was a part of this escape from the beginning. You never once believed that she was the victim—not the accomplice."

"You know there's somebody out there helping Longbow."

"Not. Melissa."

"I was wrong." Riley raised his hands. But he was surrendering to logic, not Sawyer's strong-arm insistence. "Where would a waitress get her hands on a handheld rocket launcher, anyway?"

"Sawyer." Atticus's cool head prevailed. "We need to get moving."

Loosing his grip and burying his anger deep inside with his fear, Sawyer set Holt on his feet and returned to the truck to get the rest of his gear.

Holt straightened his collar and tie beneath the vest he'd strapped on as well. He bent down to check the second pistol, strapped to his ankle. "My misjudgment about your girl-friend doesn't mean you and your clan here can take the law into your own hands."

Sawyer checked the clip in his gun and locked it in. "Somebody has to."

Atticus tightened the Velcro straps beneath his arms. "Try to think of it as us all being part of your interdepartmental task force."

"Longbow is *my* man." Holt still thought he had some chance of running this show. "If any one of you takes him, he still goes back to Jeff City with me to testify in Wolfe's trial."

Sawyer glanced up at the sky, looking for a break in the cloud cover, praying this happened fast. Once night fell, they'd have a starless, moonless night. And conducting a search in the dark would be damn near impossible.

He closed the truck door and turned to the group of about a dozen federal agents and KCPD cops. "We're going to start tracking Longbow my way. I'll give you credit,

Holt—one thing you *do* know how to do is stop traffic. Ace couldn't have gotten out of the area in a vehicle. That means he's either on foot—but with an uncooperative hostage it's unlikely he'd get very far—or, he's hiding out in one of the buildings in the area."

"I vote for choice number two," Holden quipped.

"So do I, little brother," Sawyer said. "Gentlemen? Split into teams—I don't want anyone going into a building solo. Understood? Longbow is armed and dangerous."

"My men have already conducted searches," argued Holt.

Sawyer paused before moving out. "Your men were looking for a six foot-six Native American who wants to stay hidden. We're looking for a petite blonde who wants to be found."

MELISSA WAITED until Ace's chin lolled onto his chest before she trusted that he was asleep. If she was truly lucky, all that blood matting the shoulder of his plaid shirt meant he had passed out.

Her hands were tied with the shoelace from the shoe she hadn't kicked off, her ankles bound with the panty hose she'd worn to work that morning. She'd fought him every step of the way once he'd picked her up and carried her out of the kitchen. By the time he'd dragged her up to this third-floor hideaway three blocks from the diner, his wound was openly bleeding and he was exhausted. He'd held the gun to her head to force her to remove her hose and tie her own legs, but he'd barely been able to stay awake to manage her hands, so he'd tied them in front.

In front meant she had a chance to escape.

She waited another few seconds until she heard the first snore of deep slumber. Then, working as quickly and silently as she could, she leaned over and untied the knotted hose. The open loft had the pile of burlap bags Ace was resting on—and nothing else for Melissa to hide behind if she needed to take cover.

If he awoke before she got through that sliding iron door, she'd be a sitting duck.

Did she go for the gun in his hand? Or make a run for the door?

When Ace shifted in his sleep and rolled his thigh on top of the weapon, the decision was made for her. Barely allowing her heart to beat, she slowly climbed up onto her knees and stood. She tiptoed across the floor's wooden planks, pausing at every deafening creak, cringing over her shoulder to make sure the leviathan still slept.

She made it all the way to the door before a sticky gear thwarted her escape. The rusted metal scraped and caught.

Squee. Thunk.

Her stomach twisted into that dreadful knot of stress and uncertainty that she'd lived with for three endless years when she'd shared a home with Ace. She held her breath. *Sleep. Please sleep.*

"Little one?"

Pull!

She remembered the drowsy sound of her name on his lips. Once she'd found it sexy. Now it was nothing but accusation and threat.

Melissa jerked on the handle of the door again. "Move, damn it!"

"Melissa!"

Thunder pounded on the floorboards behind her, closing in.

She pulled again, the muscles nearly bursting in her arms.

"Damn you!" Ace snatched her from behind.

Melissa screamed. "Stop it! Stop it—you're hurting me!"

He pounded on her wrists and forearms

until she lost her grip on the door. Then he lifted her by the waist and threw her across the room. Melissa remembered the sensation of flying. She curled herself into a ball and braced for the crash landing.

She hit hard, cracking her hip and shoulder on the unforgiving wood floor. Pain radiated down her arm and across her pelvis. But she had to get up. She knew to roll over and get to her feet. She stood a better chance of surviving the next blow if she was standing.

"I trusted you." He slurred the words with disappointment.

"Why? This isn't my fault. Don't make this my fault!"

"Shut up!" He advanced. She retreated.

The thunder grew louder, and she wondered if it was the storm outside or her own heart ready to burst from her chest. "I don't want to be here. I don't want to be with you." She circled around the bags and he altered course. "I have a son—*your* son—who needs me to be with him. I can't go away with you."

"I need you to take care of me."

"I don't want to."

"Like you did back in South Dakota. You were gentle to me then. I want you to love me like that again."

"I can't."

"Just come with me to Mexico. I won't have to be lookin' over my shoulder all the time down there. I'll be happy, so I won't hurt you again. I promise."

His promise meant nothing. "No."

He raised the gun and pointed it at her. "Don't tell me no!"

"I'm sorry. I…" She curled into herself, knowing she was going to run out of floor and he was going to catch her and punish her for trying to leave or for defying him—or both. She just wanted him to stop. "I'm sorry, Ace. I don't love you. You killed anything I ever felt for you."

"Melissa?" She frowned at the sound of Sawyer's voice in her head. *"You need to have faith in me."*

Another step back. Ace was closing in.

"Melissa!" Not in her head. The call was real.

Sawyer.

"I can make you love me again. But I need you to take care of me." The hand holding the gun shook, but his aim never wavered. "I think that bullet's messin' up something inside me. I need you to doctor me up and be gentle to me. Like you were back in South Dakota. We were happy then, weren't we, baby?"

She planted her feet, fighting the desperate urge to retreat from the barrel of that gun. "You're losing a lot of blood, Ace. I can't fix that. You need to go to the hospital."

She heard the soft grind of the gears at the door.

Ace heard it, too. He swung around, leveling the weapon on the intruder.

"Longbow! Drop it!"

"I'll kill her!" Ace turned his gun and lunged for her.

"Melissa!" Sawyer warned.

But she dodged Ace's grasp and swung hard with both arms. The door opened wide as she landed a roundhouse punch near the middle of Ace's chest, catching the raw, wounded flesh.

He bellowed in agony, doubling over as Melissa raced for the door. He snagged her ankle and knocked her down, but she kicked him off. She scrambled away on her hands and knees, but the threat was closing in behind her.

Then a blur of blue and white sailed past her as Sawyer attacked Ace. The battling titans rolled and cursed. Melissa slithered to a safer distance, searching for a dropped gun, calling for help, cringing at the sound of fist against bone and skull against wood.

And then it was over. Sawyer was on his feet, his mouth bloodied, his chest heaving with deep ragged breaths—with Ace's gun planted firmly against her kidnapper's skull.

"Enough, Longbow."

The obsessed giant who had terrorized her for so long was on his hands and knees, unable to catch his breath, crumpling into a sad, small shell of a man.

"You okay, sweetheart?" Sawyer called to her over his shoulder, never taking his eyes— or the gun—off Ace.

"I will be." She stood, showing him that he didn't need to worry about her. Not now. Not when he was here with her. Not when they'd made such a great team against Ace.

Making one last effort to be the big man in the room, Ace lifted his chin, staring straight into the barrel of the gun. He looked past Sawyer and smiled at Melissa. "You bitch."

"Please." There was not one drop of emotion in Sawyer's deadly calm voice. "Try something."

"No. Sawyer, please." She understood his

anger, understood the desire to punish, the need for retribution. But the violence had to end. "Don't do it. Please."

Ace laughed. "Just remember, cop. I had her first."

Sawyer's fist met Ace's cheek and her nightmare fell, unconscious, to the floor.

Sawyer swiped his palm over his mouth, wiping away the blood there. He dipped his face to the microphone clipped to his vest. "Holt. Get your ass up here. I caught your fugitive for you."

And then he pushed the gun into the back of his jeans and turned to Melissa. "Get over here. I need to see you're all right."

He never took his eyes off of Ace. Not once. He pulled out a pocketknife and quickly cut through the knots that bound her wrists. Then he pulled her arms up around his neck and picked her up, squeezing her so wonderfully tight against him that it was hard to breathe.

She heard the tramp of footsteps and shout of orders coming up the stairs, and then a swarm of armed men burst into the room. "Take him."

When they bent over Ace's body to handcuff him, Sawyer finally turned away and carried her to the door.

SAWYER CARRIED a sleeping boy into Melissa's house for the second time in as many nights. He put Benjamin to bed, kissed him good-night and, for the second night in a row, wished that this life was his.

But Melissa was walking him to the door, not inviting him to stay for coffee or forever.

He supposed that with Ace finally back in custody—in a cell-like hospital room with Riley Holt volunteering to be his new best friend 24/7 until he was physically able to be transferred to a real lockdown facility—that Melissa had no need for a six-foot, five-inch guard dog camping out on her couch for protection every night.

Probably just as well. He was beat. He was beat-up. And the filter that tempered his emotions so he wouldn't come on too strong and frighten Melissa off had pretty well been shot to hell this afternoon when he'd seen Ace pointing a gun at her head.

He loved her. Loved her family. But a few hours of feeling safe after years of feeling Ace Longbow breathing down her neck was hardly enough time for Melissa to know what she felt about any man. Hell. Maybe she'd decide that men weren't worth the trouble, and she'd take her quest for independence to the extreme.

Thanks for your help, Sawyer. Don't need you anymore. Nice to know you. Bye.

Yeah. Tonight might still be a little too early to push his feelings on her. Maybe he could settle for making a play date with Ben.

Melissa unhooked the chain lock and opened the front door. A curtain of rain fed the lake that was rapidly turning the lower elevations of the Teagueses' yard into swampland.

Her weary sigh beat him to the punch. "Somehow, I guess I thought the rain would end once Ace was captured and put away."

"It's not gonna rain forever." He reached over to brush that stray tendril off her face and tuck it behind her ear.

"Oh my God." She stepped back, frowning as she took his hand between both of hers. His knuckles were bruised, and one had split and swollen to the size of a small walnut. She angled his injuries up to the hallway light to inspect the damage. She touched the corner of his mouth, too, inspecting the bruising there. "I didn't realize how badly you were hurt."

Sure, his hand ached, but probably not as bad as the bruises on her hip and shoulder that the doctors had mentioned to him for his police report. He could have pummeled the bastard into the ground for each of those bruises, and then hit him one more time for the rope burns he'd put on Melissa's wrists. But Mel found that kind of violence distasteful, and it would only serve to remind her of Ace. So Sawyer pulled away from her touch and made a joke. "Yep, Longbow's face was about as unforgiving as a slab of concrete."

"You should have let the hospital treat you."

"Not as long as Riley Holt was there. The nurse would have had a hard time getting an accurate reading of my blood pressure."

The beginnings of a smile on her face dissipated most of the ache entirely. It seemed the most natural thing in the world to lean down and kiss her, to feel that beautiful smile beneath his lips. She was warm and wholesome and sexy and everything a man could want in a woman. But when Sawyer freed his hands from his pockets to pull her closer and deepen the kiss, she turned away.

Right. *Don't push.*

He should try that going thing again. He pointed to the darkness right outside her door. "You still need to get that porch light fixed. Just because Ace isn't a threat anymore doesn't mean that there aren't other creeps out there you need to watch out for."

"I will."

"Well…good night."

"Sawyer?"

"Yeah?"

She closed the door and fastened the locks. Then she tugged on one finger of his injured hand. "You'd better let me put some ice on that and get it cleaned up."

An ice pack, some alcohol for each other's bruises and a pair of shoulder massages later, Melissa was stretched out on top of him on the couch, and Sawyer was taking his own damn sweet time exploring all the wonderful intricacies of kissing Melissa's mouth.

He was hard, he was heavy, and if she rubbed herself against him like that just one more time, he was going to embarrass himself. But if getting to second base was all she was comfortable with yet, then Sawyer would take the double and consider himself a lucky man.

Thankful that little boys and moms with earplugs slept too soundly to hear any of this gloriously frustrating make out session, Sawyer tried to concentrate on the intriguing pattern Mel was drawing with her fingertips at his nape. But her tongue was growing bolder inside his mouth, and her hips were shifting, twisting…

Ah hell. In one fluid move that was half strength and all desire, Sawyer sat up, spilling Melissa onto his lap. But he kept right on moving, grasping the luscious curve of her bottom and lifting her as he stood. She wrapped her arms around his neck and held on as he carried her weightless body down the hall and into her bedroom, kicking the door shut before tumbling with her onto the bed.

Months of love denied and the danger of the past few days rushed together in a maelstrom of adrenaline and desire. One hand found the buttons of that shapeless waitress dress while the other tangled in her hair. He nipped the point of her chin, then supped farther down, tasting every inch until he found the bundle of nerves at the side of her throat that made her quiver beneath him.

"Tell me what you want," he whispered against her throat, catching her thighs beneath one of his and adjusting himself to a less urgent position. "I don't want to make any mistakes with you."

"Um…" Her hands were folded neatly between them.

"Mel?"

She was just lying there, her eyes closed tight…holding her breath?

Sawyer raised his head. He wasn't gonna like this. "Talk to me."

Her eyes popped open and he read the apology written there. "I don't know what I want. I mean, I want *you*." She smoothed her hand over his chest, quickly reassuring him. "But I don't know what to ask you for. I've never been with anybody except Ace. And he just kind of took charge."

That son of a bitch had worked his way between them again. Biting down on a curse, Sawyer pulled the front of her dress together. He caught his breath and ignored his zipper, ready to accept whatever answer she gave him. "Do you want to do this?"

"Desperately."

Laughing with relief at her ingenuous answer, Sawyer rolled onto the bed beside her. "You know, for the mother of a four-year-old, you have a lot to learn about sex."

Was that a laugh he heard from her? "Tell me about it. I don't know what I like or don't like. You must think I'm an idiot."

When she started to turn away from him, Sawyer caught her hand and pulled it down to the bed between them. "This could be interesting," he challenged.

"How so?"

They lay there in the dark, side by side, staring up at the ceiling. He was so crazy for the woman, he was about to bust, and yet he wouldn't have traded this intimate talk in the dark for anything.

"Think back, before Ace." The name soured in his mouth, but Sawyer quickly moved on. "Was there any fantasy you had? Any—I don't know—schoolgirl fairy tale you dreamed about?"

"You want to know about my schoolgirl fantasies?"

"It's a place to start."

"Well…I don't suppose you have a big black horse to whisk me away on. Or a tuxedo and a ballroom."

Sawyer clicked his tongue behind his teeth. "No. Fresh out of all three."

Melissa laughed, and that soft, musical sound had to be the most seductive music he'd ever heard.

"I always liked to laugh."

"Well, if I take off my clothes and you start laughing, that'll pretty much ruin the mood for me."

"That's not what I meant." He heard her gasp in the dark. "I know." Before he could ask, she rolled over, draping herself with innocent abandon over half his body, instantly rekindling the simmering desire in him. "Would you let me take off your clothes?" Oh, yeah. "I've never undressed any male except for Ben, and I hardly think…"

Sawyer raised up and kissed her. "Now you're talkin' to me."

As she climbed up on her knees beside him, he stretched out across the bed for her. "Where would you like to start?"

If only he'd known how very thorough the woman could be.

She started slow, unbuttoning his shirt and pushing it open, running her palms across his chest and stomach, then shyly bending over him to taste him with her tongue. She swirled it around one nipple, which instantly shot to attention. She squeezed a pec as she licked him again, and his stomach jerked. Her startled gasp slowly spread into a smile. "Did I do that?"

And then the wanton repeated the combination with her tongue and hand and Sawyer fisted his hands in the quilt.

"Careful, Miss Schoolgirl. There's a lot

more to this big boy that needs to be undressed."

"All right." She unsnapped his jeans and
reached for the zipper.

Before she ventured into the land of no
return, he caught her hand. "You might want
to take care of the boots first."

They laughed as she struggled with his size
thirteens. He loved how she exuded more
confidence with every move she made. And
since he hadn't made any deal about *not* undressing her, Sawyer had her stripped to
nothing more than a blush by the time she'd
rolled their protection onto him and he had
her tucked beneath him again.

Laughter aside, he captured her mouth in
a kiss, and then asked, "If anything makes
you uncomfortable... If I do anything that
reminds you of..."

"Shh." She pressed her fingers over his
mouth and he kissed each one. "He's not
going to come between us anymore. I want
you inside me now, Sawyer. This is like the
first time for me because it's the first time
I..." She tilted her chin, boldly meeting his
questioning gaze all on her own. "It's the first
time I've ever felt like an equal."

While a part of him burned at the degradation she must have endured in her marriage to Ace, Melissa was right. He had no place in bed with them. Sawyer had nothing to say more beautiful than the words she'd just spoken.

He kissed her breast, kissed her mouth, then slipped inside her. Giving her several moments to get accustomed to his size and weight, Sawyer closed his eyes and marveled at her tight, welcoming heat. They were made for this. Made for loving.

"I want you now, Sawyer. Now."

At the urgent clutch of her fingers at his spine, he moved within her and made her his.

Chapter Eleven

Melissa had never heard so much laughter in her kitchen. Somewhere between sticking spoons on their noses and falling in love, she'd finally found the fairy-tale life she'd once dreamed about.

With his free hand, Benjamin reached for another of Fritzi's chocolate-chip cookies off the counter. Melissa caught that one, too, and cleaned it with the damp cloth in her hand. "Don't get messy again."

"Need some help, Big Ben?" Sawyer reached over them both to swipe the cookie Benjamin had been denied.

"Put that back!" Melissa swatted his arm and rescued the cookie, pushing both boys away from the plate. "These cookies are to take to Mrs. Kincaid's house." She scooted Benjamin toward the front door, grabbing the cookie again when Sawyer attempted a second attack, and setting it back on the plate. "Now go on. Have Grandma help you with your jacket. I need to get these wrapped up so you can go. You don't want to be late."

"Can Ho'den play?" Benjamin asked. Sawyer's brother seemed to have moved up to the number two spot on her son's favorite-playmate list.

Sawyer took Benjamin's hand and helped him and Fritzi both put on their jackets to face the spring morning that promised even more rain. "That's right. Holden will be there. He'll play. And then your mom and I will be there a little later. But we have some things we need to talk about first."

"Now you two take as much time as you need." Honestly, could her mother's wink-wink implication get any more obvious?

Melissa's relationship with Sawyer was a pretty new thing—heck, even calling it a *relationship* was something she was still getting used to. But if Fritzi Teague had her way, there'd be wedding bells and grand-babies on the way by the end of the day.

Melissa needed to move a little more slowly. But she was moving. And Sawyer was being more patient than she'd ever realized a man could be.

"Goodbye, Mom." Melissa hurried her along before she could embarrass Sawyer—if that was even possible. She grabbed Susan Kincaid's high-school yearbooks from the stand beside the door and held them out. "Don't forget these. And tell Susan we'll be there in time for lunch."

"All right, dear." Fritzi took Benjamin's hand and walked out the door. "Come on. Your mommy and Sawyer need some time to play."

"Mother!"

Sawyer laughed at her burning cheeks, waving goodbye and closing the door and sweeping Melissa up into his arms in one smooth precision move. "You heard what the lady said. Playtime."

Melissa laughed until he stopped up her mouth with a kiss. And then she was walking backward, unhooking buttons, reaching for snaps and trying to keep her lips connected to his as she led Sawyer back to her bedroom.

At the last moment, he swung her up in his arms, carried her through the doorway and dumped her on the bed. By the time she was done bouncing, he had her jeans off and was crawling over her. His strong thighs hugged hers together. His big palm rested possessively at her hip and he was nibbling at that sensitive spot on her throat that made rational thought nearly impossible.

"Sawyer. We forgot the cookies."

"Oh, darn."

She forgot everything else as his hands moved over her, arousing things and removing the rest of her clothes. Without one whit of remorse, he kissed her senseless and filled her heart with everything she could ever ask for.

SAWYER AWOKE to the sound of pounding at the front door.

"Hell."

He had a beautiful woman in his arms, hope in his heart and a very, very bad feeling about the ringing of the doorbell and the repeated pounding.

"What's going on?" Melissa was sexy and rumpled as she sat up, pushing her tangled hair behind her ears. She was slower to revive from their morning spent "playing" together. But he could tell from the pale cast to the skin around her scar that she was worried, too.

Pulling his jeans on over his shorts,

Sawyer retrieved his gun from the top shelf of her closet and headed out the door. "Stay put."

He unlocked the front door to find his brother Holden dressed in his black SWAT gear, complete with black boots, flak vest and a very grim expression. "Don't you people turn on your phones or TV set?"

Atticus followed Holden inside. While baby brother went to the TV and scrolled through the channels to find the news, Atticus made a less dramatic, though even more disturbing pronouncement. "You'd better get dressed, Sawyer. And get Melissa out here."

But she was already there. Walking down the hallway, fully dressed, that expressionless mask firmly in place. "What's wrong? What's happened?"

"It's Longbow," Atticus explained. There was a hesitation in his normally unflappable demeanor. "He's on the run again."

Sawyer held tight to Melissa's hand when she slipped her fingers into his palm.

Holden left the special news report on the television screen. "Your buddy Holt and his men have him trapped in an old warehouse down by the river."

"Shoot him. Kill him." It wasn't the most gracious or rational of plans, but it was the only one Sawyer's gut could come up with at the moment.

Melissa sidled up against his arm. "There's something else."

"Yes, ma'am," Atticus replied. "Your mother's in the hospital with a concussion and Longbow has a hostage."

Sawyer wrapped his arm around Melissa's waist as her knees buckled.

"Benjamin."

"Yes, ma'am. He wants to trade the boy for you."

DISCUSSION ON THE SUBJECT of Melissa going into that warehouse by herself had been brief.

"No."

"Damn it, Sawyer, he's my son."

"I love him, too." Sawyer clipped his black-striped badge onto his belt so that he would be clearly identified by the federal snipers and local SWAT teams positioning themselves at various locations inside the warehouse and out. He tucked the gun that he'd probably have to lose in the back of his belt, and planted a smaller one inside his boot. While he talked, Holden checked the open channel on the two-way radio clipped to the flak vest he wore. "I'm not going to lose either one of you to that bastard. I'm going in."

Melissa looked small, huddled inside his leather jacket, but the tilt of her chin looked surprisingly strong. "But all these guns…"

Riley Holt joined them at the impromptu command center of police vans, black-and-white cruisers and unmarked cars outside the front of the building. Ace had apparently holed up in a loading-dock office adjacent to the river. "You've got my word that no one will fire as long as the boy is on the scene."

"And you've got my word that he'll keep his." Atticus's promise was more convincing.

Sawyer understood his mission. Get Benjamin safely back into his mother's arms. Period.

Anything else that happened was… There was nothing else.

"I'm ready."

"Sawyer." Melissa wound her arms around him and hugged him tight. "I want my little boy back. Ace won't care if Benjamin gets hurt."

"I do."

He kissed the crown of her hair and pushed her away.

And then he went inside.

"I SAID MELISSA had to come."

"You don't get what you want this time, Longbow." Sawyer set his gun on the floor as Ace had ordered and kicked it under the tilting, three-legged desk. Ace held his own son in front of him like a piece of body armor. Benjamin's face was splotchy from crying, but his eyes were dry now. Sawyer couldn't be prouder. Or more afraid. "You okay, Big Ben?"

"I want Mommy."

Ace laughed. "I want Mommy, too."

The big Native American seemed to have benefited from his short stay in the hospital. The color had returned to his face. And though he wore a sling over the arm that held the gun pointed at Sawyer, his strength seemed to have returned.

The cold hate in his eyes was the same.

"You'll be fine, Ben," Sawyer promised. If he died today, it wouldn't be before Benjamin Teague was safely back in his mother's arms. "I just need you to do everything I say, the instant I tell you to. Okay? It'll be like a game of Sawyer Says."

"I don't wanna play." The kid was scared. Any smart kid would be. But he didn't seem to be hurt in any way. Maybe Melissa was right—

Ace had no interest in the boy, no affection for him, no connection. So Benjamin wasn't the focus of Ace's misplaced rage and obsession. Still, with at least twenty guns trained on Longbow, and that one dangerous weapon in Ace's hand only a few inches from the boy's chest, Benjamin could be easily hurt. Or…

He wasn't going to think about the *or*.

He wasn't going to lie to Benjamin, either. "Somebody might get hurt here if you don't do exactly what I say, buddy. So will you help me?"

Benjamin nodded.

Good. Now for Ace.

"You didn't shoot me when I walked through that door. So I don't think you're going to."

"Didn't want to waste my bullet."

Sawyer might not have been so generous. "You think you've got a better chance of walking out of here with a cop as a hostage?"

"No. You're still gonna die." Benjamin squirmed in Ace's grip and Sawyer raised his hand, silently warning him to be still. "I wanted to see you suffer before putting you down. I want you to hurt the way I hurt when I heard you were sleeping with my wife."

"Enough. Ben's a smart kid. He understands what you're saying."

"He understands that you took my wife from me? That you turned her against me? He understands that you've been screwing her while claiming to be his friend?"

"Shut up."

Sawyer locked onto Benjamin's frightened eyes, willing him to understand how much he loved him, how much he wanted to be his father.

But Ace misread the silent exchange. "You wanna take another swing at me, don't you. Hell, you want to take my knife and ram it up in my gut."

Sawyer wanted to do a lot of things, but he didn't vocalize a one of them because he was certain that Ben understood the threats being exchanged. He'd worked too hard to prove to Mel that despite his size and muscle and emotional nature, he wasn't a violent man like her ex.

Riley Holt's voice whispered into Sawyer's earpiece. "The clock's ticking, Kincaid. Get the kid out of there."

For once he agreed with Holt. "Let's do this trade-off, Longbow. The deal's simple. You give me the boy, and you get to live."

"What about Melissa?"

"She's not part of this."

"She's everything."

He heard Melissa's voice in his ear. "What's happening? Why is it taking so long? They're both safe, aren't they?"

Yeah. We're going to be fine.

Time to try a different tactic. Get Longbow flustered. He wasn't a deep thinker. Shouldn't be too hard. "So how'd you do it, Ace? How did you escape from prison? How did you stay one step ahead of the feds? How did you get away from the hospital? Who's helping you?"

"You'd love to know that, wouldn't you, Kincaid." *That's it, you talk, I move closer.* "A friend needed me out of prison to do some work. That's what he does—gets men like me out to get the tough jobs done. My job was to cover the trail by taking out Hank and Tyrell after they finished their gig. Helped me get out of the hospital, too. Must have another job for me. Brilliant, ain't it?"

"What friend? Who?" Sounded more like Ace's *friend* wanted to give the con plenty of rope to hand himself. Kidnapping a child was a pretty sure bet to make Ace Longbow number one on every cop's list.

"I'm not giving you a name." He shifted his grip, moving Benjamin to a higher position on his chest. "But I've heard *your* name. I knew who you were before you ever got in bed with my wife."

"What are you talking about?" Ace was trying to turn the conversation on him. It was working.

"Kincaid. My boss is very familiar with your father's death."

"You know something about his murder?"

Ace laughed, taunting. Oh, yeah. Threaten Benjamin, drop a bombshell about his dad. This bastard deserved some major payback. "You get me out of this mess and get me and Melissa on a plane to Mexico and I'll talk."

Sawyer's stomach fisted in his gut. *What do you know about Dad's murder?*

No. Save Benjamin.

He wasn't the smartest brother, but he'd always been the one to think on his feet. "I'll consider the deal. You tell me who this boss is first."

"Don't know the name. Don't need to. I'm a free man and I get paid well."

"If you know so much, this boss isn't going to let you live. He probably helped you get away from the hospital just so the cops could kill you."

"There are a bunch of them—old friends of your father. Someone your daddy worked with."

"Who?"

Holt's voice sounded in his ear. "Get out of there, Kincaid. Let us handle it. Every man, hold your position. We're at condition red. Repeat, condition red. But hold your position until I give the order to fire."

"Who do you work for?" Sawyer demanded. "What old friends? Who killed my father?"

"Shut up."

"Give me the boy!"

"I said shut up!" Ace thrust the gun forward. He pulled the trigger.

Pain smacked Sawyer in the chest as the bullet hit his vest. He went down to the concrete, biting off his curse and rolling forward. He shoved the desk into Ace's legs and pushed to his feet as the Native American jerked back.

"Jump, Big Ben!"

The little boy kicked. Reached. Jumped. Sawyer snatched Benjamin from Ace's arm, tucked him to his chest and dropped to the floor, covering Ben with his big body.

"I have him! I have him!" he shouted, crawling toward the door to get a brick wall between them and Ace's gun.

"Move in!" Holt ordered.

The office window shattered behind Sawyer, and he glanced back to see Ace go stiff. His eyes wide open. Startled.

And then a sea of red bloomed across the front of his shirt.

"No!" Sawyer shouted. "He can tell us about Dad!"

But after the first shot, a dozen more were fired. Glass was shattering, falling.

"Who fired that shot?" Holt bellowed in Sawyer's ear. "Cease fire! Cease fire!"

There was nothing to do but hide Benjamin beneath him and ride out the storm.

SAWYER DIDN'T NEED any medicine. He didn't need alcohol for the bruise on his chest. He needed answers that Ace Longbow's death had denied him.

And he needed to see that woman and boy pushing their way through the circle of uniformed and plain clothes officers.

He dismissed the EMT tending his cuts and bruises and stood to gather Melissa and Benjamin into his arms.

He was vaguely aware of Atticus holding Riley Holt back. Something about questions can wait. All their questions could wait.

When he finally came up for air, Melissa was smiling. That beautiful smile that neither a scar nor history nor another damn cloudburst could ever dim again.

She touched her fingers to his lips in that gentle way that made him feel humble and loved and hot all at once.

"Nice guys do win." She stretched up on tiptoe again.

With the way Melissa was kissing him, Sawyer decided to revise his opinion of the weather. With Benjamin tucked securely in one arm, he wrapped the other around Melissa and pulled her up for a long, leisurely kiss that promised everything that tonight—and their future—had in store for them.

Even as the sun peeked from behind the clouds, the rain poured down on them, washing away the baggage of Melissa's life with Ace Longbow and tempering his grief over his father's death.

"Marry me, Mel."

She nodded. Smiled. Laughed.

"I'll marry you, Sawyer."

Benjamin grabbed Sawyer's chin and demanded he be included. He was. "I'll marry you, too."

"Done."

His father would approve.

* * * * *

Look for Atticus Kincaid's story,
ARMED AND DEVASTATING,
next month.
Only from Harlequin Intrigue.

Brooke twisted her hair up and reached for the clip that would anchor it to the back of her head. So much for the boost of confidence the new suit and glasses were supposed to give her as she started work at the Fourth Precinct today. Not that she wasn't excited about the transfer to newly promoted Major Mitch Taylor's office. She was going to be administrative assistant to the man now in charge of every watch and department in the Fourth Precinct offices. She loved the challenges of her career, thrived on making her professional world run efficiently. Working with computers and data, an attention to facts and details—those were definitely strengths of hers where her confidence could truly shine.

Her comedic-sidekick looks weren't the real issue this morning.

The new job wasn't what was making her heart race and her mouth dry.

Even Major Taylor's tough and gruff reputation as a demanding boss didn't really worry her.

It was Atticus Kincaid. *He'd* be there.

Brilliant detective. Tall. Black haired. Capable of turning her into a stuttering idiot with a direct look or a teasing remark. Two weeks of working side by side with him, poring through his late father's files—searching for a lead on John Kincaid's murder and finding nothing useful—had taught her that embarrassing lesson. His broad shoulders and crisp style did wonders for a suit and tie—and frustrated her hormones no end.

Not one of her smartest moves—developing a crush on a man who looked at her like a kid sister or his father's frumpy secretary. There was a date that was never gonna happen.

Though she and Atticus wouldn't be working in the same office, they'd be working in the same building, possibly on the same floor. No doubt she'd bump into him in the break room, or have to sit across from him at a meeting table.

How was she supposed to be competent and professional around him without getting her crowded thoughts and well-meaning words twisted up inside her throat? Chances were her new coworkers would think she was dim-witted or indifferent or just plain stuck-up before she could help them understand how thrilled and honored she was to be there and to be a part of their law enforcement team.

And the most embarrassing part of it was that Atticus would be patient and polite no matter how badly she and her shy genes fumbled around.

He was as good a son to her former boss, John Kincaid, as all the Kincaid boys had been. And, like the rest of his family, he'd been sweet enough to check on her a couple of times at John's funeral three months ago— even though she'd repaid him with bruised knuckles and mud on his sleeve. She had always been so grateful for the Kincaids' kindness to her.

For John Kincaid's sake, she'd bury her misguided attraction and slug her way through her social awkwardness and make a success of herself at the Fourth Precinct.

For John.

* * * * *

The editors at Harlequin Blaze have never been afraid to push the limits—tempting readers with the forbidden, whetting their appetites with a wide variety of story lines. But now we're breaking the final barrier—the time barrier.

In July, watch for *BOUND TO PLEASE* by fan favorite Hope Tarr, *Harlequin Blaze's* first ever historical romance—a story that's truly Blaze-worthy in every sense.

Here's a sneak peek…

BRIANNA stretched out beside Ewan, languid as a cat, and promptly fell asleep. Midday sunshine streamed into the chamber, bathing her lovely, long-limbed body in golden light, the sea-scented breeze wafting inside to dry the damp red-gold tendrils curling about her flushed face. Propping himself up on one elbow, Ewan slid his gaze over her. She looked beautiful and whole, satisfied and sated, and altogether happier than he had so far seen her. A slight smile curved her beautiful lips as though she must be in the midst of a lovely dream. She'd molded her lush, lovely body to his and laid her head in the curve of his shoulder and settled in to sleep beside him. For the longest while he lay there turned toward her, content to watch her sleep, at near perfect peace.

Not wholly perfect, for she had yet to answer his marriage proposal. Still, she wanted to make a baby with him, and Ewan no longer viewed her plan as the travesty he once had. He wanted children—sons to carry on after him, though a bonny little daughter with flame-colored hair would be nice, too. But he also wanted more than to simply plant his seed and be on his way. He wanted to lie beside Brianna night upon night as she increased, rub soothing unguents into the swell of her belly, knead the ache from her back and make slow, gentle love to her. He wanted to hold his newly born child in his arms and look down into Brianna's tired but radiant face and blot the perspiration from her brow and be a husband to her in every way.

He gave her a gentle nudge. "Brie?"

"Hmm?"

She rolled onto her side and he captured her against his chest. One arm wrapped about her waist, he bent to her ear and asked, "Do you think we might have just made a baby?"

Her eyes remained closed, but he felt her tense against him. "I don't know. We'll have to wait and see."

He stroked his hand over the flat plane of

her belly. "You're so small and tight it's hard to imagine you increasing."

"All women increase no matter how large or small they start out. I may not grow big as a croft, but I'll be big enough, though I have hopes I may not waddle like a duck, at least not too badly."

The reference to his fair-day teasing was not lost on him. He grinned. "Brianna MacLeod grown so large she must sit still for once in her life. I'll need the proof of my own eyes to believe it."

Despite their banter, he felt his spirits dip. Assuming they were so blessed, he wouldn't have the chance to see her thus. By then he would be long gone, restored to his clan according to the sad bargain they'd struck. He opened his mouth to ask her to marry him again and then clamped it closed, not wanting to spoil the moment, but the unspoken words weighed like a millstone on his heart.

The damnable bargain they'd struck was proving to be a devil's pact indeed.

* * * * *

Will these two star-crossed lovers find their sexily-ever-after?
Find out in BOUND TO PLEASE
by Hope Tarr,
available in July
wherever Harlequin® Blaze™
books are sold.

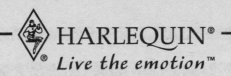

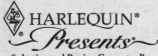

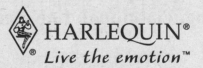

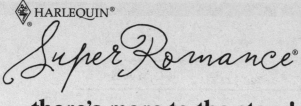
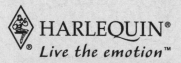

HARLEQUIN®
Presents

**The world's bestselling romance series...
The series that brings you your favorite authors,
month after month:**

Helen Bianchin...Emma Darcy
Lynne Graham...Penny Jordan
Miranda Lee...Sandra Marton
Anne Mather...Carole Mortimer
Susan Napier...Michelle Reid

and many more uniquely talented authors!

Wealthy, powerful, gorgeous men...
Women who have feelings just like your own...
The stories you love, set in exotic, glamorous locations...

HARLEQUIN®
Presents
Seduction and Passion Guaranteed!

Harlequin® Historical
Historical Romantic Adventure!

Imagine a time of chivalrous knights and unconventional ladies, roguish rakes and impetuous heiresses, rugged cowboys and spirited frontierswomen— these rich and vivid tales will capture your imagination!

Harlequin Historical . . . they're too good to miss!

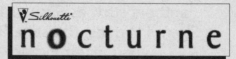